'I LOVE LOVE LOVE *Lucky Six*!'
Jasmina, age 8

'*Lucky Six* is the best series EVER! Aimi is my
favourite character cos she is bad and gets away
with it, but only sometimes'
Zoe, age 11

'Elle, Noah, Laurie, Jack, Marybeth and Aimi are all
brilliant, imaginative characters with very adventurous
personalities. Laurie wants to be a detective. The idea of
the mysterious piano and the box inside it is amazing!'
Sophie, age 10.

'Laurie is the greatest cos she's got the same name
as me and I like solving mysteries too'
Lauren, age 11

'If this series was a cartoon I would watch it loads'
Courtney, age 9

LAURIE

NAME: Laurie Hunt

AGE: 14

NATIONALITY: British

STUDYING: Singing, drama

ROLE IN LUCKY SIX:
Lead singer and songwriter

PERSONALITY: Inquisitive

INSTANT-MESSAGE NAME: LuckyStar

JACK

NAME: Jack Hunt

AGE: 12

NATIONALITY: British

STUDYING: Music

ROLE IN LUCKY SIX:
Bass guitarist

PERSONALITY: Cheeky

INSTANT-MESSAGE NAME: CaptainJack

AIMI

NAME: Aimi Akita

AGE: 13

NATIONALITY: Japanese

STUDYING: Music

ROLE IN LUCKY SIX:
Lead guitarist and wannabe singer/songwriter

PERSONALITY: Outspoken

INSTANT-MESSAGE NAME: RockChick

MARYBETH

NAME: Marybeth Fellows

AGE: 13

NATIONALITY: American

STUDYING: Music, dance

ROLE IN LUCKY SIX:
Keyboard player

PERSONALITY: Caring

INSTANT-MESSAGE NAME: CurlyGirly

ELLE

NAME: Elle Beaumont

AGE: 14

NATIONALITY: French

STUDYING: Singing, dance

ROLE IN LUCKY SIX:
Band manager and backing singer

PERSONALITY: Very efficient!

INSTANT-MESSAGE NAME: ElleB

NOAH

NAME: Noah Hansen

AGE: 14

NATIONALITY: American

STUDYING: Music, drama

ROLE IN LUCKY SIX:
Drummer

PERSONALITY: Laid back

INSTANT-MESSAGE NAME: DrummerDude

SASHA

NAME: Sasha Quinn-Jones

AGE: 13

NATIONALITY: British

STUDYING: Dance

PERSONALITY:
A snooty show-off who's got it in for Lucky Six

CHELSEA

NAME: Chelsea Woods

AGE: 13

NATIONALITY: British

STUDYING: Dance

PERSONALITY:
Sasha's sidekick – with more talent in her little finger than her friend has in her entire body . . .

Chapter One

Miss Diamond is probably our favourite teacher at The Verity Lang Academy and not just because she's a big fan of our band, Lucky Six, either. OK, so she drives us around to our gigs and is totally great when it comes to giving us advice about the entertainment industry, but she's also really careful not to play favourites. She's the singing teacher and vocal coach at the academy and a total inspiration to us students. She's young, too, which means she knows what we're talking about when it comes to music – unlike some of the older members of staff and – dare I say it – our parents! And she's pretty cool as well with loads of curly caramel-coloured hair and blue eyes. We always love the trendy clothes she wears. Trust

me, she is the *last* teacher we would want to upset. But one morning, during a vocal training lesson, we managed to do just that.

So, there we were in class, with Miss Diamond playing a tune for us all to sing along to and it should've been easy enough but, unfortunately for us, the piano was so ancient the song was completely unrecognisable.

Now, Elle and I normally take Miss Diamond's lessons very seriously and we know how important practice is but today . . . well, we just couldn't concentrate because of the strange piano music. It was just so funny! And you know what it's like when you get the giggles? You just can't stop, and Elle and I kept catching each other's eye. Every time I opened my mouth to sing Elle pulled a silly face and every time *she* opened her mouth *I'd* do the same. I really don't know what got into us.

Each time a duff note rang out, we'd giggle and it didn't take Miss Diamond long to notice what was going on. She stopped playing immediately, a look of surprise on her face at our bad behaviour.

'Lauren!' she shouted, glaring at me and using my full name – which she never normally does. 'And Elle. I'm surprised at you – really I am.'

We both went bright red.

'You're completely disrupting the class.'

I thought that was totally unfair because I knew that everyone had found it really funny – and they'd probably been giggling too – but just hadn't been caught. Annoying, huh? But I thought better not make a scene about it.

'Sorry, Miss Diamond,' I said instead, looking at the floor, aware that all eyes were on me from around the piano.

'What were you both laughing about anyway?'

I looked up at her. 'It's the piano, Miss Diamond,' I said. 'It sounds terrible! You must've noticed. It's so old. It really needs replacing.'

Miss Diamond looked at me a second longer. Then, 'Elle?' she asked, and Elle nodded in agreement. 'Well,' she continued, 'that's as may be but your horseplay is costing everyone else valuable vocal-training time. You give me no option but to

3

give you a half-hour detention after lessons today to reflect on your behaviour.'

'Yes, miss,' I said quietly with a sigh.

'Yes, miss,' Elle said.

'In the meantime, I think an apology to the rest of the class would be a start,' Miss Diamond said.

'Sorry,' I said, in a low sort of a mumble.

'Sorry,' Elle echoed.

The lesson continued and Miss Diamond did her best with the ropey old piano. Elle and I sang along with the rest of the class and I had to admit that the awful-sounding tunes just weren't that funny any more.

Later that day, after lessons, Elle and I arrived for our detention.

'What a total drag,' I said.

'I can't believe I've got a detention,' Elle said, pushing a strand of her perfect glossy brown bob behind her ear. 'I've never been to detention in my life!'

'Oh, Miss Perfect!' I said, secretly thinking it funny that our very own band manager and 'Miss Organisation' had landed herself in trouble. 'It wasn't *my* fault so don't blame it all on me.'

'I'm *not* blaming it on you,' she said.

'Yeah, sounds like it.'

'I'm not, Laurie, *really*.'

'You were giggling just as much as I was.'

'I know,' she said. 'That piano sounded so funny.'

I nodded and couldn't help grinning at the memory of it. 'It's really terrible, though,' I said. 'We shouldn't be laughing about it. It should be replaced – and soon. Before it collapses or causes us all to sing out of tune.'

We started giggling again.

'It was making me sing all wrong,' I said.

'Me too,' Elle said. 'As if I had a toad in my throat.'

'A *frog*!' I said. Elle – who's French – is always getting little things like this wrong.

We laughed again – until we saw that Miss Diamond had pulled out two tables and chairs for us to sit at from the pile stacked at the back of the room. And she'd set them a good distance apart so there was no chance of us getting distracted and chatting instead of sitting there in silent boredom.

'Come along now, girls,' she said, nodding to the chairs.

'Well, I guess I'll see you later,' I whispered to Elle as I chose the table and chair to the left of the classroom.

Elle groaned quietly. 'I swear I'll never giggle *ever* again.'

I smiled hopelessly and we took our seats on opposite sides of the room.

Have you ever noticed how time can play tricks on you? When you're having a good time – like when we're rehearsing with our band and everything's going really well – the time will rush by and, before you know it, it's time to go to a boring old maths class. But then, when you're struggling over some terrible page of equations and really have no idea if x equals two, three or five hundred and twenty, time just crawls along. Well, sitting there in the silent classroom was one of the instances when time wasn't in a hurry, which was a real nightmare for me because I'm such a fidget. I just hate being still. It's not natural. I like to be doing something – *always*. So, there I was, sitting like a dope, crossing and uncrossing my legs, examining my fingernails, twisting my hair and making tiny circles with my fingertips on the desk but *still* the time didn't seem to be passing.

I guess we must have been about halfway through our boring old detention when there was a knock on the door and Ms Lang, our headmistress, popped her head round. Ms Lang, in her sixties now, was once a famous ballet dancer and I felt totally bad about her seeing me in detention.

'Lauren?' she said, spotting me first. I smiled and nodded towards my fellow sufferer. '*Elle?*' she said, even more surprised to see her there. 'What are you both doing in here so late?'

'Detention, Miss,' I explained.

'*You* two?' she said, obviously shocked that we should be in trouble.

We watched as Ms Lang's little white poodle, Mister Binks, nudged the door open, tail wagging, and headed towards us. He's a bit of a star at the academy. Most people love him and he loves most people. Apart from one of our teachers, Mr Walsh, who – for some reason known only to Mister Binks – he snaps at whenever he gets the opportunity.

I reached down to give him a fuss, his curly coat warm and comforting.

8

'Hello, Mister Binks,' I said, and he looked up at me with his big dark eyes, obviously enjoying the attention.

'Ah, Miss Diamond,' Ms Lang said, as she noticed her. 'I must say, I'm very surprised to find these two in here.'

'Yes, Ms Lang,' Miss Diamond said with a sigh, which made me feel guilty all over again. 'So am I, but I didn't have a choice, I'm afraid.'

'Really?' Ms Lang looked curious and disappointed all at once.

'Yes, they both had a fit of the giggles during their vocal-training lesson this morning and completely disrupted the class,' Miss Diamond said.

'Oh, dear,' Ms Lang said. 'And what caused that, may I ask?'

Miss Diamond cleared her throat and looked a little embarrassed, as if she were afraid of telling the truth. 'The piano.'

'The piano?'

'Yes, Ms Lang. Mr Walsh has had a look at it for me but he says it's beyond tuning. It really has seen better days, unfortunately.'

'I see,' Ms Lang said with a strange sort of smile. For a moment, I imagined Ms Lang as a teenage girl, totally sure that she too would have been giggling uncontrollably at the sound the piano had made that morning. 'Well,' she continued, 'I'm sure you'll all be rather pleased with my news, then.'

I looked across the room towards Elle and she shrugged.

'One of my dear old friends,' Ms Lang said, and, as she said the word *friends*, I couldn't help noticing that her face lit up, 'Monsieur Philippe Montpellier, the French pianist, has left his fabulous piano to me in his will.'

Miss Diamond's eyes widened at the news and I exchanged glances with Elle again.

'And I would be very happy to donate it to the vocal training classroom,' Ms Lang concluded, with a broad smile. 'It will look wonderfully at home here, I'm sure, and I know you will take very good care of it.'

'Oh, Ms Lang!' Miss Diamond said, getting up from her chair. 'This will solve all our problems. It's very generous of you. And you can be sure that we will cherish it.'

Ms Lang waved a hand dismissively in the air as if her gift were nothing really – like she gave pianos away every day of the week.

Elle and I got up from our seats too in the excitement, completely forgetting that we were still in detention.

'Isn't that great news, girls?' Miss Diamond said.

'Brilliant!' I said, nodding enthusiastically.

'Yes, thanks, Ms Lang!' Elle said.

'Just think,' I giggled, 'no more duff notes.'

'No more appalling scales,' Elle laughed.

'And no more inappropriate fits of giggles,' Miss Diamond said, trying to hide a smile.

Elle and I nodded. It was really cool. We couldn't wait for the new piano to arrive.

Chapter Two

'Hey, if it's not my favourite detention dude,' said Noah, sliding into the seat next to me and Marybeth. I felt myself blushing the same shade as the ketchup I was squeezing on to my plate. OK, so I should probably admit that I have a massive crush on Noah. And, so far, he's shown no sign whatsoever of returning my feelings. But a girl can dream, right?

'I still can't believe it,' said Jack, grinning as he tucked into his sky-high pile of mashed potatoes. 'My sister, otherwise known as Little Miss Perfect, in detention. A dear-diary moment if ever there was one.'

I flinched as a dollop of potato catapulted straight from his mouth on to my nose. 'Say it, don't spray it, Wart-face,' I said, flicking the potato right back at him.

'Seriously, though,' said Aimi, leaning forward, 'what was it like? Did you have to write lines? Did Miss Diamond smack you across the hand with a ruler as you wrote to make sure you got the message? Did she threaten to give you the slipper?'

I stared at her. 'Honestly, Aims, I wonder about you sometimes. You've seriously been reading far too many old books about boarding schools. Can you really imagine Miss Diamond hitting us? Besides, it's completely against the law for teachers to hit children and I should know, my parents are . . .'

'Police officers!' the others groaned.

'Well, they are!' I said huffily, folding my arms. And that's no doubt where I get my love of solving mysteries from.

'They're my parents, too,' said Jack, 'but you don't hear me banging on about it, do you?'

I poked my tongue out at him.

'Oh, very grown up,' he snorted. 'I don't know how I'm ever going to live up to having you as a big sister.'

'So,' said Aimi quickly, before me and Jack could really start squabbling. 'No ruler, no slipper. Hmm. Did Miss Diamond shout at you till you cried?'

'No, Aimi,' I sighed, in exasperation.

'Well, what *did* happen, then?' she asked.

'Basically, we just had to sit in silence and think about what we'd done.'

Aimi sat back in her chair, looking disappointed. Jack rolled his eyes. 'Lame. Bring back the cane, that's what I say. A quick whack on the bum would soon sort out disruptive influences like you and Elle.'

'Yeah, right, Jack,' I said. 'You'd never be able to sit down again if they brought back the cane. You're always in trouble for messing around in class.'

'Whatever, big sis,' he said. 'I wasn't the one in detention.' He nodded wisely. 'Well, I hope you've learned your lesson. You let Miss Diamond down, you let the academy down, but most of all you've let yourself down.'

Younger brothers! You can't live with them, you can't kill them.

'So,' said Noah, 'did Miss Diamond let you off early on account of her being such a big Lucky Six fan?'

'I wish,' grimaced Elle. 'I've seriously got to get some laundry done. And it's far too late to put a load on now. It's so unfair. I'm already having to wear my skankiest clothes.' She sighed heavily and glanced down at her totally pristine top. I rolled my eyes. Honestly, the girl is so well turned out she'd make the Queen feel scruffy.

Noah was staring at her as if she had suddenly started talking in a foreign language. Mind you, to Noah the word laundry might as well be part of a different language. The boy isn't exactly a clean freak. I looked fondly at his creased T-shirt which, if I wasn't mistaken, he'd been wearing for the last four days.

I dragged my mind back to the subject in hand.

'One interesting thing did come out of detention, though,' I said.

'You realised your behaviour wasn't big or clever,' said Jack.

I kicked him under the table.

'No,' I said. 'We're getting a new piano for the vocal-training studio. Ms Lang came in to tell Miss Diamond while Elle and I were there.'

'In detention,' added Jack, in case anyone had forgotten.

'How come?' said Marybeth.

'Laurie and Elle disrupted class, so they had to stay behind . . .'

'Funny,' said Marybeth. 'I meant, how come we're getting a new piano?'

'One of Ms Lang's friends left it to her in his will. I've no idea who this friend is, but Ms Lang actually blushed when she was talking about him.'

'Apparently, her *friend* was French,' chipped in Elle. 'And you know what they say about French men . . .' She arched her eyebrows knowingly.

17

'What?' said Aimi. 'That they come from France?'

'That they smell of garlic?' added Jack.

'No,' said Elle huffily, studying her perfectly styled hair in the reflection in her knife. 'That they are very rrromantic.' She rolled the 'r' for extra emphasis. 'And I should know – I am French, after all.'

I noticed no one gave her a hard time for reminding us that she was French, like they had me for simply pointing out that my parents were

police officers. Mind you, Elle was so good looking that no one ever gave her a hard time about anything. I felt my shoulders droop. Sometimes life just wasn't fair.

Jack made gagging noises. 'Thanks, Elle,' he said. 'Now, I've got pictures of Ms Lang getting romantic with some French man in my head!'

Noah cuffed him playfully round the ear. 'Jack, now we've *all* got pictures of Ms Lang getting romantic in our heads!'

Aimi shook her head and stood up. 'And on that *lovely* note, I'm off. I've got homework to do. Plus I want to check out the latest gadget my parents have sent me.'

Aimi's parents work in communications technology (otherwise known by Aimi as gadgetry). They're always sending her the latest thing in Japanese mobile phones, MP3 units, gaming and computers. Her room looks like something out of *Star Trek*.

Waving over her shoulder, Aimi strolled towards the door. Noah and Jack exchanged a

19

glance and stood up as well. 'We've got homework to be getting on with too,' said Jack.

I raised an eyebrow – my little brother was not known for his keenness to get on with his school work. 'And by homework I presume you mean a computer game that needs playing.'

Noah and Jack looked sheepish. 'Well, maybe just a quick game,' said Noah, pushing his hair back off his face. I couldn't help but notice the cute way his sandy curls flopped back into place.

'Yeah,' said Jack. 'It'd be rude not to.'

The pair of them headed off. Marybeth looked thoughtful and glanced at me. 'How come the vocal-training room is getting the new piano? I mean, the one in the main music room isn't too hot either. You'd think, with the amount of money students pay in fees, there'd be more money for new equipment.'

I shrugged. 'I guess keeping a school this size going must be pretty expensive.'

'I'll tell you exactly what the problem is,' said a voice behind us. Sasha Quinn-Jones. Year-nine school prefect, talent-free zone and complete troll. 'All our fees go towards paying for spongers who can't afford to pay for a decent education.'

She leaned in towards Marybeth and smiled nastily, her blue eyes like chips of ice. 'Oh, sorry, Marybeth. I didn't see you there. No offence.'

She stepped back, smirking, as Chelsea Woods – Sasha's best friend, clone and total yes-woman – giggled pathetically.

Marybeth flushed to the roots of her hair, her bottom lip trembling. Sasha Quinn-Jones has a real thing about Marybeth. Unlike a lot of the students at The Verity Lang Academy, Marybeth's family aren't incredibly rich or famous, which meant she got into school on a scholarship based purely on her amazing talent. And, seeing as the admission standards for the academy are amongst the highest in the country, that's pretty impressive. For some reason, Sasha thinks her family's wealth gives her the right to be nasty to Marybeth and anyone who hangs out with her. Well, I for one wasn't going to put up with it. I stood up, giving

Marybeth's shoulder a protective squeeze. Sasha's eyes narrowed, watching me.

'You know, the real problem is that they let the odd talentless witch into the academy. But, hey, at least it gives the rest of us a laugh,' I said. 'Oh, sorry, Sasha,' I said. 'I didn't see you there. No offence.'

Sasha stalked off, Chelsea hurrying behind her, as Elle burst out laughing.

'That told her,' I said. I looked at Marybeth who still looked a little watery round the eyes.

Elle put her arm round her. 'Take no notice,' she said.

Marybeth tried to smile. 'Let's talk about something else,' she said.

'I've got some news that'll cheer you up,' Elle beamed. 'My mum's invited all of Lucky Six over to Paris at half-term!'

'No way!' I gasped. Elle's mum is an incredibly well-respected French journalist, and Elle lives with her, her stepdad and stepbrother, Christophe, in France during the holidays. 'That'll be amazing.

I've always wanted to go to Paris!'

'Think how much fun we're going to have!' Elle grinned. 'I can show you all the good places that the tourists never find.'

'I can't wait.' I hugged her. 'It's going to be brilliant.'

I glanced at Marybeth, who, to my surprise, didn't look the least bit cheered up by the news. Sasha's words must really be bugging her. I slung my arm round her shoulders.

'Don't worry about Sasha Witch-face Quinn-Jones – she's so not worth it.'

Marybeth stared fixedly at the floor, and shuffled her feet uncomfortably.

'Oh, that's not why I'm upset . . .' She paused and took a breath. Her face crumpled slightly and I could tell she was struggling not to cry. Concerned, I looked at Elle, who shrugged helplessly back at me. 'It's just that I spoke to my mom last night and she was worrying about money. There's no way I can ask her to pay for me to go to France. She just can't afford it.'

Me and Elle gave her a huge hug.

'We've got a bit of time before half-term,' I said. 'Maybe we'll be able to think of some way of getting the money.'

'Thanks.' Marybeth tried to smile. I noticed it didn't quite reach her eyes. 'But I don't think it's going to happen. I've already had to ask Mom to get me some new tap shoes. Mine are totally worn out. Even if I did manage to raise the money, I'd feel terrible spending it on a vacation when Mom's trying to scrimp together the cash for me to have some shoes.'

I gave her shoulder a squeeze. 'It won't be the same without you,' I said.

'It certainly won't,' said Elle, kissing her on both cheeks. 'We'll miss you.'

Marybeth smiled bravely. 'Enough already, you two. You'll make me cry. And I don't know about you guys, but I've got math homework to do.'

That's the thing about stage school – however talented you are, it just doesn't get you out of normal homework. More's the pity.

Chapter Three

You might imagine that at the end of a half-term everything slows down. But at stage school the total opposite is true. Teachers hand out homework like there's no tomorrow and not just maths and English. Oh, no. We're all expected to keep up our dance, singing, music and acting training, too. So, by the time Elle and I walked into our last vocal-training class before the holidays, we were practically bent double under the weight of our bags crammed full of assignments. It was quite a relief to find Miss Diamond standing beaming at us from in front of a new piano. Her blue eyes were dancing as she clapped her hands for silence.

'Ladies and gentlemen,' she said, 'I'd like to

introduce you to a new addition to our class.' She gestured to the piano.

'There's a seat free next to me,' said Dan Piper, budding comedian and Noah's best friend, 'if the new addition would like to sit down.'

The class giggled as Miss Diamond rolled her eyes good-naturedly.

'This isn't just any piano,' she went on, as the laughter died down. 'It's a Grölmeister, one of the most expensive and best makes of piano to have been produced in the twentieth century. We're incredibly lucky to have it here at the academy. Especially as a member of the Montpellier family contested Philippe Montpellier's wish to leave it to Ms Lang.'

'Ooh, Philippe!' I mouthed to Elle.

'Ms Lang's lurrrrrrrve,' she whispered back. I stifled a giggle.

Miss Diamond was still speaking. 'Fortunately, that's all been resolved and the piano is at last in its rightful place – here at the academy. Gather round for a closer look.'

27

Now, I might not know as much about musical instruments as Aimi, Jack and Marybeth, but even I could tell this piano was something pretty special. Its deep, dark wood was polished to a high sheen. Miss Diamond carefully wiped her hands on her combat trousers and sat down at the piano. She rested her fingers for a minute on the keyboard, then began to play, her caramel curls bobbing along in time. The sound that filled the room was rich and resonant. I grinned at Elle. This was a world away

from the terrible out-of-tune banging that the old piano had produced. One thing was for sure, our vocal training had never sounded so good.

An hour later, Miss Diamond reluctantly closed the piano lid. 'That's enough for today,' she said. 'Well done, everybody. Make sure you keep practising during half-term. Now, it may be the holidays, but there's one thing I want you all to make time for . . .'

I rolled my eyes at Elle. Not more homework. Please.

'And that's to make sure you have lots of fun!' Miss Diamond grinned at us. 'Class dismissed.'

The class cheered. No wonder the whole school loved Miss Diamond so much. As Elle and I piled our stuff into our bags, she wandered over.

'So, girls, now we have a new piano I don't expect to see either of you in detention ever again,' she said.

I flushed a fetching shade of bright red. 'No, miss,' we muttered, staring fixedly at the floor. I was still upset about having been in detention

with Miss Diamond. Even by academy standards, she's the coolest. Almost not like a teacher at all. I hated to think that she might still be annoyed with me.

'Good,' said Miss Diamond. 'Having an out-of-tune piano is no laughing matter, especially when everything you play sounds barmy rather than Beethoven.'

I looked up to see Miss Diamond grinning at me. I smiled back, relieved. Something told me we were definitely forgiven for our attack of the giggles.

'A-hem. Sorry to interrupt, Miss Diamond.' Mr Walsh was standing in the doorway, a middle-aged man next to him carrying a bag that was even bigger than mine. 'This is Charles Morris, a piano tuner from Morris and Co. and he's come to tune the piano.' Mr Walsh walked towards the Grölmeister and ran his hand lovingly over the closed keyboard lid. 'What a beauty. I expect she needs a bit of TLC after her long journey from France.'

He opened the keyboard and ran his fingers over the keys, closing his eyes and swaying slightly. 'Lovely,' he said. Mr Walsh is an ex-concert pianist who now plays accompaniment for all the dance classes.

'I'll leave you to it.' Miss Diamond smiled. 'I've got a couple of things to see to. Laurie, Elle, I'll see you later.' Gathering her stuff together, she hurried out of the room.

'See you later, Mr Walsh,' I said, as I headed out with Elle. But Mr Walsh was still lovingly stroking the piano, the tuner fidgeting impatiently next to him, and didn't hear me.

Walking down the corridor, we bumped into Marybeth coming out of her dance class with Mrs Walsh.

'We've just left Mr W.' Elle grinned cheekily at Mrs Walsh. 'He's in love with the new Grölmeister. He was meant to be showing the piano tuner where it was, but the poor man couldn't get a look in.'

Normally, we'd never dream of talking to a teacher about her husband like this, but Mrs Walsh is different. An ex-dancer, she's firm but fair in class, pushing her students to the highest

standards, but outside of lessons she's almost like the academy's resident mum, especially as far as the boarders are concerned.

Mrs Walsh smiled. 'Oh, believe me, Elle, I know all about it. He's been itching to get his hands on it. He couldn't believe his luck when the piano tuner turned up asking for directions during class. Apparently Ms Lang had given him clear directions over the phone as to exactly where the piano was, but somehow he still managed to get lost.'

She grinned at us. The Verity Lang Academy is a complete nightmare if you don't know your way around; it's like a massive rabbit warren. Years ago, before it became the school we all know and love, the main academy building used to be a hospital. When I first started here, I used to have seriously bad dreams about getting lost and never finding my way out.

'Obviously Robert was only too happy to show him the way, if it meant he could have a tinkle on its ivories. Well, I'll leave him to it. I'm off to the staff room for a cup of tea. Have a good half-term, girls.'

I grinned excitedly at Elle. 'This time next week, we'll be at your house in Paris. Can you believe it? I can't wait. Oh!' I stared at Marybeth, who was smiling bravely. 'I'm so sorry! I can't believe you're not coming too.'

'Neither can I,' said Marybeth. 'I mean, I've stayed at the academy in the holidays before and there are always plenty of other boarders here, but this is the first time that none of you guys will be around with me. And to make it even worse I've just found out that Sasha's going to be staying as well!'

I felt terrible. 'Look,' I said, 'why don't I stay? It's not fair you have to be here on your own. I can always go to France another time.'

Marybeth smiled. 'Thanks, Laurie, but no way are you missing out because of me. You just have to make sure you stay in touch – I expect constant updates.'

I reached into my bag for my mobile and tapped out a quick text message.

Missing u already xx

A few moments later Marybeth's phone let out a beep. She checked it and grinned. I saw her type a message back.

Right back at u xxx

Somehow I knew Marybeth would be just fine without us.

Chapter Four

Later that evening, I lay on my bed, running through what had gone on during the day. I had a funny feeling I just couldn't shake that something wasn't quite right. What was it? I ran through the big events.

Leaving Marybeth? Nope, that wasn't it. I mean, obviously I felt weird about it. But that wasn't what was causing the feeling that I'd missed something.

The huge amount of homework I'd been set? Well, yes, obviously I should be making a start on the stack of schoolwork I'd been given. After all, the sooner I got on with it, the quicker it would

35

get done. And, yes, I probably shouldn't be lying on my bed right now, but should be at my computer making a start.

Sighing, I rolled off my bed and switched on my laptop. As I started tapping on the keyboard, I couldn't help laughing as I remembered Mr Walsh at the Grölmeister. Bam! There it was, that funny feeling again. What was causing it? Suddenly I knew. It was the fact that the piano tuner had been left to wander around the rabbit warren that is The Verity Lang Academy by himself. No way would Ms Lang leave a stranger to find their own way to the vocal-training studio. Even if she was too busy, surely she would get the caretaker, Mr Brown, to show him the way. Ever since a first year got lost for two hours before anyone found her, Ms Lang has made it school policy that students have to act as guides to new-starters and visitors to the school. So, how come the piano tuner had been left to his own devices? It didn't make sense.

Rubbing my nose, I clicked on the Internet icon

and did a search for Morris and Co. A few minutes later, I found their web site. It was seriously flashy. The company logo took up most of the home page and around it were images of some really expensive-looking pianos. There were also loads of very complimentary comments from satisfied clients. I quickly clicked through. By the look of things, they had some very high-brow customers. I clicked on the 'About Us' page where there was information about the company and biogs of the staff. I looked closely at the list of names: Ian Morris, David Morris and, yep . . . Charles Morris. For a moment, I'd wondered if he'd been an impostor, but it looked like Morris and Co. were completely above board. I couldn't shake the feeling that something wasn't right, though. Charles Morris had seemed rather dodgy, the way he'd stood fidgeting behind Mr Walsh. But, to be fair, maybe that had been because he just wanted to do his job rather than listen to Mr Walsh play the piano. After all, if you're surrounded by amazing pianos every day, they probably end up losing their appeal a bit.

I felt slightly disappointed. Then I shook my head at my thoughts. What was it with me? Would I really rather that the piano tuner was actually a criminal mastermind roaming the school looking for his next big job?

I idly typed 'Grölmeister' into the search box, averting my eyes guiltily from the enormous pile of homework that was in danger of toppling off my desk. I meant to get on with it. But somehow sleuthing always has the edge over homework. I can't help it. I guess that's what happens when you have police for parents. It's in the blood.

But despite my best efforts I didn't find anything that interesting, only that a Grölmeister always has a distinctive maker's mark stamped somewhere inside the body of the piano. I stared closely at the image. I was going to make sure I looked for that tomorrow when Lucky Six used the vocal-training studio for a rehearsal. Normally, we'd just use one of the practice rooms, but Marybeth wanted to try out the piano. As the keyboardist in Lucky Six she was gagging to get her hands on something as special as a Grölmeister. And at least pointing out the mark meant I wouldn't look like a complete musical-instrument dunce in front of the rest of the band.

Closing down the computer, I reached for my French homework. After all, I was about to head to France, so there was really no excuse. But after twenty minutes of translating a passage of French back into English, I could feel my eyes starting to close. Sighing, I closed my book and fell into bed. When I dropped off to sleep, shadowy figures filled my dreams and in the background a piano played a haunting melody.

The next day, I headed into the vocal-training studio at lunchtime for band practice. Marybeth was already seated at the Grölmeister.

'This piano is really great,' she said. 'Shame we can't use it all the time. Just think how good we'd sound.'

'It's a bad workman who blames his tools,' said Jack, looking up from plugging in his bass.

Marybeth (sensibly) ignored him. 'Now, if Noah would just hurry up, we can get on with practice.'

'Hey, did I just hear my name taken in vain?'

I felt my heart do a back-flip as I turned to see Noah grinning in the doorway.

'Sorry I'm late,' he said, doing one of those

flippy things with his drumsticks. You know, twirling it, like it was a gun and he was an outlaw in a Western. The boy was born to be a rock star. 'I had a collision with the marching brass band. They were practising their formations. Mr Hooper had a right go at me.'

Typical Noah. I grinned back at him as he leaped on to the stage and settled in behind his drum kit.

'Well, now we're finally all here, can we please get on with rehearsal?' said Aimi. 'We've only got an hour. Laurie, can you move your microphone stand over a bit? It's blocking my light.'

I rolled my eyes. I love the girl to death, but, if she had her way, she'd be onstage by herself, with the rest of us playing and singing from the wings. Total diva.

Band practice went brilliantly. Especially the last song, 'All Aboard', which is Marybeth's favourite and I dedicated it to her as a kind of *au revoir* until we were all together again at our next band rehearsal after half-term.

'That,' said Elle, 'was excellent.'

41

'Yep!' Jack grinned. 'No one was out of tune, or out of time and – even better – no one stormed out.'

I stuck my tongue out at him. I have to admit, I do have a history of storming out of band rehearsals, usually after an argument with Aimi. What can I say? It might not be the most professional behaviour, but it's certainly rock 'n' roll.

Exhausted, but elated, we started packing up. I filled the others in on my research the night before. Aimi sighed.

'Seriously, Laurie,' she said, 'you need to get a grip. You're looking for mysteries where there aren't any.'

'Yeah,' said Jack. 'The biggest thing you've come up with is whether the piano has a mark on it or not. I mean, who cares? Boring!'

'Well, at least I didn't waste my night shooting zombies on some mind-numbing computer game,' I sniped back.

'We'll all be zombies if we have to listen to any

more of your uninteresting stories,' said Jack. 'Have you met my sister? Laurie Boring, from Dullsville, Snoretown, postcode ZZZ ZZZ.'

'Shut it, Wart-face,' I said.

'You shut it, Snores-brain,' he said.

'No brain.'

'Dur brain.'

'Takes one to know one.'

'Shut up!' shouted Aimi. There was an awkward silence while Jack and I glowered at each other.

'I wish I hadn't said anything now,' I muttered.

'Don't we all,' said Jack.

'Actually,' said Marybeth, 'I think it's quite interesting. I wonder where the mark is.' She opened up the piano and peered inside. One by one, we all went over to look.

'Come on, Jack,' said Noah, sliding under it to try to spot the mark. 'Get involved.'

'Do I have a choice?' he moaned.

We all looked at him. 'No,' I said. Muttering under his breath, he slouched over.

'There it is!' said Elle, pointing to the side of the

43

piano. We all stared at the mark, clear as day, on the inside of it.

'Well, at least we know the piano's not a fake,' said Noah.

'Whoop-dee-doo,' complained Jack. 'Remind me to memo Laurie about getting a life.'

'And while you're at it send me the memo on why it's illegal to kill younger brothers,' I said, picking up my stuff and getting ready to leave the room in a serious huff.

'Hang on a minute, guys,' said Marybeth, who was on her knees staring under the piano. 'What's that?'

We gathered round her. There, attached to the inside of the body of the instrument, was a tiny wooden box. Marybeth crawled underneath the piano for a closer look. She reached up to open it.

'It's locked,' she said.

What on earth was it? We all stared, transfixed.

Chapter Five

'What do you think is in it?' asked Marybeth.

'I don't know, but I think we should find out,' said Jack.

I nudged him in the ribs. 'Not so boring now, eh?' I said.

Aimi grinned. She put out a hand, whipped a hairgrip out of Marybeth's hair and started bending it out straight.

'Ow!' said Marybeth, her hand clutching at the spot on her head where the clip had been. 'What are you doing?'

'I've seen people opening locks with hairgrips on TV. How hard can it be?'

She darted forward under the piano and started

poking the lock with the pin. The hairgrip promptly snapped in half and pinged across the room, almost hitting Elle in the eye. Aimi sat back on her heels, and frowned at the lock.

'Noah, give me your credit card,' she demanded, holding out her hand.

'Aims, I'm fourteen years old,' said Noah. 'I don't have a credit card.'

'Oh, yeah, right,' said Aims. She leaped up and tried to pull another grip from Marybeth's head.

'Ouch!' Marybeth screeched, her hands pressed to her head again. 'Seriously, Aims, calm down.'

'Yeah, get a grip!' sniggered Jack. 'Get a grip! Geddit?!'

'Well, we've got to get this box open somehow!' said Aimi. She dived under the piano again and started pulling viciously at the lock.

'Stop it!' shouted Marybeth, yanking the back of Aimi's school skirt. 'You're going to ruin the piano!'

At that moment, the bell rang for class. Aimi climbed reluctantly back out from underneath the Grölmeister.

'Typical!' she said, looking at her watch. 'I've got to get to class. How about we all meet back here after school?' Casting one last reluctant look back at the box, she hurried out of the room. The others quickly followed behind her, Marybeth still rubbing her head.

'Talk about being saved by the bell.' Noah winked at me as I crouched down, still staring at the box. 'We'd better hurry or we'll be late for drama.'

I blinked at him. I'd been so distracted by the box that I'd almost missed the fact that I was alone with Noah.

Almost, but not quite.

'Here's your bag,' he said, holding it out for me. OK, so it might not be a sign of undying love, but at least it shows he cares. Right?

'What do you think is in the box?' Noah asked, as we hurried along the corridor and up the stairs to the drama studio.

I rubbed my nose. 'I really don't know.'

'What if it's something really gross like nail clippings?'

I stared at him. For a smart guy, Noah could be surprisingly clueless sometimes. Cute, but clueless.

'Noah, why would there be nail clippings in a locked box?'

'Well, maybe the pianist cut his toenails at the piano seat, shoved them in the box, then locked it so they didn't fall out during performances.'

I shook my head in disbelief. Fortunately, we'd arrived at the studio so I didn't have to answer.

'Laurie and Noah, stop dawdling and come inside. Class is about to start,' ordered Mrs D'Silva, her heavy bracelets jangling as she beckoned us in.

'Right, everyone, warm-up exercises,' she cried, pinning up her dark hair with a pen. 'I want you all to make the following sounds, mi mi mi mi mi, mo, mo, mo, mo, mi, mo, mi, mo, mi mi mi mi, mo, mo, mo. And remember to open your mouths as far as they will go.' We all obediently started making the noises, while pulling faces that, quite frankly, would frighten small children.

'Right, everyone,' said Mrs D'Silva. 'Keep on making the noises, but, while you do, I want you to start moving around the room, becoming a different animal every time I clap. Ready? Go.'

We all started to move. I became a cat, a monkey, a giraffe, then an elephant. Each time, I tried to put my all into the exercise, but I couldn't stop thinking about the box. I was obviously doing a better job than Noah, however.

'Noah Hansen, what on earth are you meant to be?' Mrs D'Silva asked, as he came to a confused stop, scratching his head.

'An anteater,' he said.

'And since when have anteaters stood still scratching their heads?' Mrs D'Silva asked him.

'Well, actually that was me being me. I realised I didn't have a clue what anteaters do, apart from the obvious stuff like eating ants,' he answered.

Mrs D'Silva sighed as the rest of the class giggled. I felt a bit sorry for her. Noah is totally talented, but he can be incredibly unfocused.

'Right, everyone, stand in a circle. I want you all to do some improvisation, so let's play Pass the Prop.'

I groaned inwardly. Pass the Prop is where you get handed an object and have to pretend it's something else, until another person gets an idea and takes over from you. Mrs D'Silva handed one of the class a walking stick and it quickly became a sword, then someone else took it and pretended to be Luke Skywalker with a light sabre. Then Dan ran forward and grabbed the walking stick and held it to his ear, like you would a mobile phone and said, 'Sorry, I can't hear you – I've got a

51

walking stick stuck to my head.'

Everyone doubled up laughing. Even Mrs D'Silva looked like she was trying not to smile.

'Right, now, I want you all to get in pairs with the person next to you. Each pair will take it in turns to come to the front of the class and improvise a scene based on a sentence I'll give you. Roxie and Zack, you're up first. Your sentence is, "Spring is in the air."'

I sidled up behind Noah and tried to get his attention, desperate to work out what we were going to do about opening that box. He was completely engrossed in watching Roxie and Zack, though, and totally oblivious to my attempts to speak to him. Unfortunately, Mrs D'Silva wasn't.

'Laurie Hunt,' she said severely, 'I shouldn't have to remind you how rude it is to talk during someone else's performance. I would have thought you of all people would know better than to disrupt someone's class, especially after your recent detention with Miss Diamond. Let's hope you won't have to stay after class with me as well.'

I blinked back tears; Mrs D'Silva can be pretty scary when she wants to be. Shaking her head and looking truly disappointed in me, Mrs D'Silva turned away and apologised to Roxie and Zack for having to make them stop. Noah nudged me in the ribs, crossed his eyes and gave me a goofy smile. I smiled back at him sheepishly, totally embarrassed by looking like an idiot in front of him. For the rest of the lesson, I tried my best to focus on what Mrs D'Silva was telling us, determined not to get into trouble again.

When the class ended, I rushed to get my bag, still mortified by being told off. As I slunk off into the corridor, Noah came up behind me, and slung his arm casually round my shoulders.

'Don't worry, Laurie,' he said, giving my shoulder a little squeeze, 'you know Mrs D'Silva's bark is much worse than her bite. She'll have forgotten all about it by next class.'

I blushed with pleasure. Noah. Hansen. Was. Hugging. Me. Fortunately, it was mega-warm in the corridor. There's a radiator that, despite Mr

Brown's best efforts, never turns off and always pumps out blisteringly hot air whether it's summer or winter. My red cheeks could easily have been taken for the fact that I was overheating, not because I was going weak at the knees. Well, that's what I was hoping anyway.

'I've decided what we should do,' I said, trying to keep my voice from shaking.

'About what?' he asked.

I sighed. 'You'll never make a detective, Noah.'

Noah stared at me blankly. 'A policeman? Why would I want to? Dude, I'm going to be a rock star.'

My heart plummeted. Guys who are head over heels in love with a girl don't call them dude, do they? Once again, I reminded myself that Noah and I are just friends. I mean, Noah's made it completely clear that he only cares about me as a friend. Well, insofar as he's never shown any sign of returning my crush, at any rate.

'The piano, Noah. I've decided what we should do about the box.'

'Oh, yeah. The box.' He nodded thoughtfully. 'What do you think we should do?'

'Tell Ms Lang, of course. It's her piano, after all.'

Noah gave my shoulder an even bigger squeeze. 'You, kid, are a genius.'

OK, so it wasn't exactly a declaration of undying love. But it'd have to do.

Chapter Six

Meet me outside Ms Lang's office at
the end of lessons. We've got 2 tell her.
C U there Lx

When I made it to Ms Lang's office, the others were all there. Except for Noah who, of course, was late. That boy would be late for his own funeral. The excitement in the air was so intense you could almost feel it.

'Ms Lang's not here yet,' said Marybeth. 'I haven't been able to concentrate all afternoon. I just keep thinking about that box.'

'I still think you should have let me have another go at it,' said Aimi, eyeing Marybeth's hair. Marybeth backed nervously away.

'Oh no you don't,' she said. 'My scalp still hasn't recovered from earlier, thank you very much.'

'Wuss,' said Aimi.

'I got a text from Noah,' said Jack. 'He reckons the box has toenails in it.'

'What?' said Elle. 'Why would there be toenails in the box?'

'Don't ask,' I said, raising my eyes to the ceiling. 'Believe me, you don't want to know. I seriously wonder what goes on in that boy's head sometimes.'

'I bet you do.' Marybeth grinned.

I shot her a look. The last thing I wanted was for Jack to join in on the teasing. Fortunately, he'd pulled his mobile phone out of his pocket and was lost in a game.

'Sorry!' mouthed Marybeth.

'Here's Ms Lang,' said Elle.

We all turned to watch her approach. It didn't matter how many times I saw her making an entrance, whether into a classroom or onstage or even walking down a corridor like she was now, it was always obvious why she'd been such a great dancer: her poise was perfect. Today, she was wearing a tasteful grey cashmere jacket and skirt, her hair pulled up into a perfect chignon, her cane tapping across the parquet floor. Mister Binks was trotting obediently behind her. She was every bit the star.

'Well, if it isn't Lucky Six,' she said. 'Or should I say Lucky Five?' she corrected herself, noticing Noah's absence. 'To what do I owe this pleasure?'

Her voice was warm and welcoming, but there was no disguising the authority in her eyes. Ms Lang might be one of the most approachable headmistresses in the world, but one thing was for sure: you didn't mess with her.

'Hey, guys, wait for me!' Noah came bounding down the corridor, his bag flying behind him. Mister Binks yapped delightedly and ran towards him, launching himself into the air. Still running, Noah put his arms out to try and catch Mister Binks, promptly tripped over his shoelace and went flying, eventually coming to a skidding out-of-breath halt

at Ms Lang's feet. Mister Binks happily licked Noah's face. Ms Lang raised an amused eyebrow.

'Always one to make an entrance, I see, Mr Hansen,' she said, smiling down at him as everyone cracked up laughing.

'Er, Ms Lang?' I said. 'We really do need to speak to you.'

Ms Lang turned towards me, her smile disappearing as her eyes searched my face.

'Of course, Laurie.' She pushed open her office door. 'Why don't you all come inside?'

Ms Lang moved behind her enormous mahogany desk, motioning for us all to take a seat. As Mister Binks settled into his wicker basket, she slowly lowered herself into her chair, steepling her fingers under her chin.

'So, how can I help?' she asked.

'Well, it may be nothing,' I said, 'but I had a bad feeling about the piano tuner. I can't explain why – he just seemed dodgy somehow. The others thought I was being silly.'

'Not silly,' said Elle, 'just a bit mystery obsessed.'

'*Totally* mystery obsessed!' muttered Jack.

I decided that punching your younger brother in front of your head teacher wasn't a good idea and carried on with the story.

'Anyway, I decided to do a bit of research on the company last night. I couldn't find anything out of order, but I did find that all Grölmeisters have a special mark. So after band practice I told the others and we decided to look for it earlier.

Marybeth found it.'

'Yep.' Marybeth nodded. 'But that's not all I found. Tucked away by the mark is a tiny box. We tried to look inside, but it's locked.'

'So we thought we should tell you,' I said. 'It just seems strange.'

Ms Lang leaned back in her seat and looked at us all one by one.

'Thank you for telling me,' she said, looking back at me. 'You have a good instinct, Laurie; never lose it. Always make sure you listen carefully to it, despite what anyone else might say.'

It took all my will power not to stick my tongue out at Jack and shout, 'Na na na na na!' But I'm not that immature. Well, OK, I am, but I didn't want Ms Lang to know it.

Ms Lang was still speaking. 'I did book Charles Morris of Morris and Co. to come and tune the piano. But he cancelled yesterday morning. Now he may have had a last-minute change of mind and turned up without letting me know, but Morris and Co. strike me as an incredibly professional company. I think we can dismiss that as unlikely, which means there was some stranger purporting to be Charles Morris wandering our halls. The question is why?'

I stared at the others. 'It must be to do with what's in the box!' I said.

'Totally,' said Elle. 'We've got to find out what's inside.'

Aimi nodded excitedly. 'If you'd just let me have another go with . . . Ouch!'

Marybeth nudged her sharply in the ribs. Bragging to your headmistress about trying to open the box with a hairgrip really wasn't a good idea.

Noah looked at me and sighed. 'I guess that's my toenail theory out of the window.'

I took a deep breath. 'Noah, for the last time, why would anyone be interested in someone's skanky old toenails?'

'Unless . . .' Jack interrupted. 'It's a famous person's toenails.'

Noah's face lit up. 'Yeah. Stuff like that goes for megabucks on Internet bidding sites.'

'Boys,' I spoke through gritted teeth, 'believe me. Whatever's in the box it's not someone's toenails.'

'You don't know that,' said Jack.

'No, you're right,' I said. 'But I'm willing to bet on it.'

'How much?' said Jack.

'If it turns out to be someone's toenails then I'll never call you Wart-face again,' I said.

Jack's head whipped round. 'Really?'

I sighed. 'It's never going to happen. Wart-face.'

'Girly swot.'

'Oh, good comeback,' I said. 'How long did it take to come up with that?'

'Oh, cos wart-face is *such* an intellectual term.'

Elle glared at us. 'Focus, people, focus. We need to work out how to get into the box.'

Ms Lang held her hand up for silence. When Ms Lang directs, you obey. Instantly, we all stopped talking. 'Miss Beaumont is right. And I think I might have the answer.' She opened a drawer in her desk and started rifling through.

'I *know* I put it in there!' she murmured to herself, shutting the drawer and opening another one.

'Put what, Ms Lang?' asked Elle.

Ms Lang looked up at us. 'Well, along with the Grölmeister, Monsieur Montpellier sent me a tiny key. There was no explanation with it, and for the life of me I couldn't work out what it was for. But maybe, just maybe, it opens the box. But where has it gone?'

We watched impatiently as she stood up and moved away from her desk, opening the lid of an old writing desk by the window and peering inside.

'To be frank, it could be anywhere,' said Ms Lang. 'I think the best thing is if you show me exactly where the box is. You never know, maybe we'll be able to open it without a key.'

I saw Aimi open her mouth to mention the hairgrip technique. Quickly, I stood up and stepped hard on her foot.

'Ouch!' she complained.

I smiled sweetly. 'Good thinking, Ms Lang.'

Once inside the studio, we pointed out the box to Ms Lang. Putting on her spectacles, she slowly lowered herself to the floor and peered underneath the Grölmeister.

'It's made of exactly the same wood as the piano,' she said. 'I'd never have spotted it.' She leaned forward for a closer inspection. 'It's also incredibly difficult to get to. I don't think we

should try to open it without the key; we might damage the piano.'

Aimi let out a howl of frustration. 'Not if you've got small hands, Ms Lang. I could get to it. Easily!' Her hand started to snake towards Marybeth's hair.

'No, I don't think so, thank you, Aimi,' said Ms Lang, standing up and brushing her hands over her knees. 'I think the best thing to do is to call a locksmith.'

'But . . .' said Aimi.

'No,' said Ms Lang. 'A locksmith is definitely the answer. I'll ring one now. Thank you for your help. I will let you know what happens.'

We were well and truly dismissed.

Chapter Seven

The usual last-day-of-term chaos greeted me as I headed down for breakfast the next morning. There were cases everywhere, and excited students were lined up along the windows at the front of the building, watching the main entrance as if they were waiting for Hollywood superstars to arrive. Which, of course, they were. That's the thing about being at stage school: you never stop being star-struck by other people's parents.

In the canteen, I piled my plate with bacon, scrambled eggs and tomatoes, and headed over to where the others were already digging into their breakfast. Noah looked far from his usual happy self.

'What's up?' I asked, as I slid into the seat opposite him.

Noah rolled his eyes and shrugged.

Concerned, I looked at the others.

'He's been followed around by half the school all morning. Everyone's desperate to know if his parents are coming,' explained Elle. Noah's parents are Greg Hansen and Michelle Albright. Basically *the* biggest stars in Hollywood right now; you couldn't pick up a newspaper or magazine without reading something about them.

'Everywhere I go someone stops and asks me. It took me twenty minutes just to get to the canteen,' sighed Noah.

Just then a bunch of first years walked towards our table. They spotted Noah and started nudging each other.

'You ask him,' I heard one of them say. Noah buried his head in his hands.

'Not again,' he groaned. 'I can't take it!'

Jack grinned and reached into his bag.

'Here, I got you something, mate. Thought sit

might come in handy.'

He tossed a T-shirt across the table at Noah, who unfolded it and started laughing. 'Cool,' he said. 'Total genius.'

'What is it?' asked Aimi.

Noah stood up and pulled the T-shirt over his head. On the front of it was written:

No, my parents aren't coming today

Noah turned round and showed off the wording on the back:

Don't bother asking

The six of us cracked up. My brother might be a complete and utter pest, but he definitely has his moments.

'Right,' said Elle. 'We'd better get a move on. Miss Diamond said she'd meet us outside in ten minutes.'

Miss Diamond had offered to drive us to

Lowfield Station so we could get the train to King's Cross where we'd be catching the Eurostar from nearby St Pancras.

'I'm so excited,' squealed Aimi, as we all stood up.

'Me too,' said Noah.

'Me three,' I said, grinning goofily.

'Group hug!' shouted Jack, launching himself at us, knocking us over.

'Get off, Wart-face!' I grumped, as I picked myself off the floor. 'You always have to take it too far.'

'Honestly, Jack. I'm going to have to change my top now; it's ruined,' said Elle, brushing an invisible speck of dirt off her jumper.

As we walked out of the canteen, I slung an arm round Marybeth.

'How are you doing?' I asked.

She shrugged. 'OK. I mean, I'd be lying if I said I didn't wish I was going with you, but I'll be fine. Plus,' she smiled, 'Ms Lang has said I can use the Grölmeister as much as I like during half-term.

I can't wait. And at least it'll keep me out of Sasha Quinn-Jones's way.'

I hugged her. 'We'll miss you,' I said. 'It won't be the same without you.'

'You'd better believe it,' she grinned, nudging me. 'Now, go get your stuff, before I do something really wet like cry.'

Ten minutes later, we were outside trying to fit all our cases into the back of the school minivan. Or the Lucky Six tour bus as we prefer to call it. It might as well be – Miss Diamond uses it to drive us to all our gigs.

'Aimi, you do know we're only going for a week, don't you?' complained Noah, as he and Jack struggled to lift her third bulging suitcase into the van.

'Be prepared, that's my motto,' Aimi said.

'Yeah,' snorted Jack. 'Be prepared never to carry your own suitcases.'

Me and Marybeth exchanged amused glances.

'I'm going to miss you so much,' I whispered, flinging my arms round her.

'We all will,' said Elle, throwing her arms round the pair of us. Aimi and Noah joined in.

'Group hug!' shouted Jack. But this time we were ready for him, and neatly sidestepped as he launched himself at us, leaving him sprawling on the ground.

'Hey, Jack,' Marybeth laughed. 'Enjoy your trip!'

'Hilarious,' muttered Jack.

'I thought so,' said Marybeth, grinning. 'Seriously, though, I'm not good at goodbyes, so I'm going to

head in now. Have a brilliant time and make sure you keep in touch. I expect daily updates.'

As Marybeth started to walk away, Noah whipped out his drumsticks. Counting us in, he started tapping out the familiar beat to 'All Aboard', Marybeth's favourite Lucky Six song, on the side of the minivan. Linking arms we all launched into an *a cappella* version. Marybeth turned round and smiled.

'I love you guys!' she shouted. '*Au revoir!*' Waving over her shoulder, she disappeared up the stairs into the academy.

'I thought I recognised those dulcet Lucky Six tones.' We turned to see Ms Lang smiling at us.

'Before you head off, I just wanted to make sure that you know to text Miss Diamond once you're on the Eurostar train. I know you've done the journey many times before, Elle, but that's the only way I can agree to you all travelling unaccompanied to Paris.'

'Yes, Ms Lang,' we chorused. 'Of course.'

'Ms Lang? Did you manage to get hold of a locksmith?' asked Aimi. 'If not, I think I could still get that box open.' She glanced at her watch. 'There's still time before we have to catch the train.'

That's Aimi – never one to let things go.

Ms Lang raised an eyebrow. 'Thank you for your kind offer, Aimi, but that won't be necessary. I was hoping to catch you all before you left. I know how excited you are about what was in the box . . .'

We all leaned forward.

'The locksmith came last night and managed to open the lock. Strange, really. He seemed to think someone had already tried to force it. You wouldn't know anything about that, would you?'

We all shuffled uncomfortably and stared at the ground. Ms Lang raised her other eyebrow.

'No, I thought not. Anyway, this is what was inside . . .' She reached into her tiny black handbag and pulled out an expensive-looking ring box. Inside was a gorgeous gold ring, encrusted with diamonds that sparkled and glistened in the sunlight. Tucked inside the box's lid was a note. Ms Lang took it out and unfolded it, holding it out so we could read it.

Ma cherie, Verity,

I think you know in what high regard I always held you. But what you might not have known is that I have always been in love with you. I knew it from the first time I saw you onstage in Swan Lake. But I could never muster the courage to tell you how I felt. A decision I have regretted all my life. This ring is for you, Verity. It has been passed down through generations of Montpelliers and its last, rightful resting place is with you. I should warn you that others in my family will not agree with this decision. As you know, my brother Jean-Paul is an embittered, angry man, especially since my mother left only the house to him in her will. But this ring belongs to you, Verity. I only wish things had been different.

Yours always,
Philippe

'That is the most romantic letter ever!' I breathed.

'I know!' whispered Elle, reaching for my hand. Aimi nodded. For once, lost for words.

Noah and Jack rolled their eyes.

Ms Lang smiled sadly. 'Philippe was a dear and special man. Normally, I wouldn't dream of sharing such a personal letter, but if it hadn't been for all of you, I'd never have found the ring. Thank you.' She tucked the letter back into the box and placed it in her handbag. 'I must get this to the school safe. Have a good holiday. I'll see you all next term.'

I watched her walk away. She paused for a minute, and I could have sworn she was wiping her eyes, but a moment later she was greeting some parents who'd just arrived to collect their child, her professional smile firmly back in place.

My brain was pulled back to the present by the beeping of a horn. Miss Diamond leaned out of the minivan window. 'Come on, you lot. You've got a train to catch!'

An hour later, we were settled on the Eurostar, still caught up in Ms Lang's story.

'It's so romantic,' Elle sighed. 'Do you think Ms Lang was in love with him too?'

'Definitely,' said Aimi. 'It's like something out of a movie.'

'Chick flick,' said Jack, through a mouthful of cheese and onion crisps.

'Totally,' said Noah, nodding.

'You're very quiet, Laurie. You OK?' asked Elle.

I rubbed my nose. 'I've got a theory about the so-called Charles Morris. I think he's got something

to do with Philippe's brother Jean-Paul.'

Jack groaned and threw his crisp packet at me, sprinkling cheese-and-onion crumbs over a decidedly unimpressed Elle. 'Oi, Detective Hunt,' he shouted. 'You're on holiday or hadn't you noticed?'

I decided to be the bigger person and ignore him. Not easy when you've got bits of cheese-and-onion crisps in your hair. Pulling my mobile out of my bag, I texted Marybeth to update her on what Ms Lang had told us.

A few minutes later, my phone beeped.

> Mr W says p tuner coming again 2mrrw
> 2 take piano away cos he didn't have
> right tools 4 job!!! MB xx

I stared at the text. Why would the piano tuner have to take the piano away? Surely it was just a simple case of returning with the right tools? Alarmed, I showed the others. Aimi shook her head at me.

'Laurie. Ms Lang already knows about the piano

tuner. She'll have sorted it and this will be a proper one. Stop worrying about it and enjoy yourself.'

The others nodded their agreement.

'Yeah, Laurie, you're making a mountain out of a moleskin!' added Elle.

I couldn't help grinning as Jack began to explain why it was a molehill not a moleskin, I stared out of the window. I knew something was up. I just knew it.

Chapter Eight

Finally, we arrived in Paris. Elle's mum – Madame Beaumont – and Elle's younger stepbrother, Christophe, were waiting for us outside Customs.

'Cherie!' she shouted, as she spotted Elle. The pair of them hugged for ages, chattering excitedly in French. Finally, Mme Beaumont broke away and greeted the rest of us in perfect English.

'I am so excited to have you all here. It will be lovely to spend some proper time with all of Elle's friends. I normally only get to see you in school showcases. It is such a shame that Marybeth couldn't be here too. You will miss her, no?'

'Definitely,' we nodded.

'OK, to the car,' Mme Beaumont said. 'It's parked

just outside.' She eyed Aimi's pile of suitcases nervously. 'I just hope we can fit all of your things in. Thank goodness it's a people carrier.'

Ten minutes later, we and our luggage were all installed in the car. Mme Beaumont's driving left a lot to be desired. I hung on to Aimi's arm as we swerved round corners, while Mme Beaumont chatted away, gesturing while she spoke. To take my mind off her driving, I leaned forward to ask a question.

'I was wondering, do you know anything about the Montpellier family? Philippe and Jean-Paul? I think Philippe was a famous concert pianist.'

As Mme Beaumont turned round in her seat to look at me, taking her eyes completely off the road, I almost wished I hadn't asked. But when she answered I was glad I had.

'Ah, yes, the Montpellier family. They are very famous. The family are well known in France. Of course, Philippe is known throughout the world; such a sad loss to music. There was a big scandal ten years ago. I remember writing about it for the

newspaper I was working for at the time.'

'What was the scandal?' I asked.

Mme Beaumont turned to look at me again and I made up my mind not to ask any more questions. I wanted her to keep her eyes on the road in front of us, for all our sakes.

'Well, it was well known that Philippe and Jean-Paul didn't get on. They never had, ever since they were little children. The relationship, er, how you say, became more bad, as they became men. Philippe showed huge potential as a pianist whereas Jean-Paul could never settle to anything and was happy to live on money given him from his *mère*, sorry, his mother. But it became even worse when their mother died, and they . . .'

Mme Beaumont asked Elle something in French.

'Quarrelled,' said Elle.

'Ah, *oui*,' said Mme Beaumont. 'You must excuse me; my English is not as good as it was.'

'It's brilliant,' I said. 'I wish I could speak another language as well as that.'

Mme Beaumont turned round to beam at me and the car swerved across the road. I gripped Aimi's arm even tighter.

'Where was I?' she said. 'Ah, *oui*, Philippe and Jean-Paul, they quarrelled over the will. Jean-Paul thought he had been treated unfairly: he was left the ancestral home to look after, while Philippe was left priceless paintings and jewellery.'

'What's unfair about being left an ancestral home?' asked Jack. 'I wouldn't say no to one of those.'

Mme Beamont looked questioningly at Elle, who quickly translated, then she laughed.

'Ah, but you are imagining something *très grande, non*? This house was very big but also, um, how you say, very neglected. It needed a lot of money to keep running. I think Jean-Paul's mother hoped it would give him something to focus on and would be the making of him. Sadly, this was not true. Jean-Paul was already jealous of his brother's fame and fortune, but now he became even more bitter. He talked to a lot of journalists, I was one of them, and said very bad things about his brother. He wanted people to think badly of Philippe.'

'That's terrible!' said Elle.

'I know,' said Mme Beaumont. 'But his plan, it did not work. The whole world could see what he was trying to do, and in the end public opinion turned against him. No one came to see the house – they did not want to pay their money to such a bitter man – and he was left with no income. It was very sad really. The house was beautiful in its day. His mother would be so sad to see it if she was still alive. It's not far from here, and every time I see it, I feel so sad, imagining him living there, bitter and alone.'

'Near here?' I said. 'Do you think we could stop and have a look?'

Elle, Aimi, Noah and Jack all groaned.

'*Mais bien sûr*, Laurie,' said Mme Beaumont. 'It would be my pleasure to show it to you. I only wish Elle would take such an interest in French culture.'

Elle rolled her eyes, forgetting her mother could see her in the rear view mirror.

'Honestly, Elle,' said Mme Beaumont, shaking her head at her daughter. 'You don't hear your brother complaining, do you?'

'Only because he has no idea what we're all saying,' Elle retorted. 'You know he can't understand English!'

Leaning forward she spoke rapidly to her brother in French, gesturing at her mother and me. Christophe let out a huge groan and slumped down in his seat.

'See!' said Elle, sitting back and folding her arms. Mme Beaumont muttered under her breath.

'Great holiday so far,' Jack hissed at me. 'Good one, Laurie.'

I stuck my tongue out at him.

Five minutes later, Mme Beaumont indicated right and swerved across the road, startling a couple of rabbits who sensibly ran for cover. She drove down what must once have been a grand drive but was now overgrown with weeds. We pulled up outside a ramshackle mansion. You could see it must once have been beautiful, but now it just looked sad. The paint was flaking off the doors and window frames, and ivy covered most of the house.

As we piled out of the car, an old woman opened the door and barked at us in French. Mme Beaumont stepped forward and after a brief conversation she beckoned for us to join her.

'This is Mme Lameme, Jean-Paul's housekeeper. Apparently, Jean-Paul is abroad on urgent business, so she's agreed to show us around the house. I don't think she's very happy about it though.'

'Brilliant!' I said. 'That's really nice of her.'

'Brill-i-ant,' muttered Jack.

'Sarcasm really doesn't suit you,' I said, as Elle's mum and Mme Lameme disappeared inside.

'No, looking round boring old houses really doesn't suit me,' he retorted. 'Just because you've got some crazy idea about Jean-Paul doesn't mean you have to ruin all our holidays!'

'Looking round one house hardly counts as ruining everyone's holiday!' I said.

The others all shuffled their feet, looking uncomfortable. But I noticed none of them agreed with me.

'Whatever, sis. Let's just get this over with, shall we?'

Feeling slightly hurt, I hurried to catch up with Mme Beaumont who was standing in the hallway with Mme Lameme, who looked pointedly at our shoes as we walked inside and growled an instruction at us in French.

'Can you all take your shoes off, please?' said Mme Beaumont.

Obediently, we all stepped out of our shoes.

'Like it's going to make any difference,' Elle muttered, looking in distaste at the decidedly worn carpet. 'I've never seen such a disgusting carpet. And what is that awful stink? It smells like something's died!'

'Er, sorry.' Noah grinned sheepishly. 'I think that's my feet.'

Trying not to laugh at the appalled expression on Elle's face, I looked around the hallway. The inside of the house was in an even worse state than outside. Faded wallpaper was hanging off the walls, the paintwork was scuffed and chipped and what little furniture there was wouldn't have looked out of place in the local charity shop.

Mme Lameme led us into the huge living room, still chuntering moodily in French. Mme Beaumont pointed at huge patches on the walls where paintings must once have hung and asked something in French. Mme Lameme let out a short barking laugh and answered. I looked at Mme Beaumont questioningly.

'I asked if Jean-Paul had to sell the paintings to raise money for keeping the house. But they were paintings that were left to Philippe in their mother's will. Apparently, Jean-Paul could never afford to replace them.'

I looked around the room. There was still one painting left in the room, hanging over the ornate fireplace. I stepped closer for a better look. It was obviously a family portrait. Two handsome middle-aged men stood either side of a much older, but still beautiful woman.

I pointed at it. 'Who's that?' I asked.

Mme Beaumont turned to the housekeeper, who started chattering away in French. Mme Beaumont listened, nodded, then walked over to me.

'That is a portrait of Madame Montpellier, Jean-Paul and Philippe. It was painted shortly before her death.'

I stared at the painting. Could it be . . .?

'I wonder,' I said out loud.

'What was that, dear?' said Mme Beaumont.

'Oh, nothing.' I smiled at her. 'I'll catch up with you in a minute.'

As the others left the room, Jack dragging his feet across the faded carpets, I reached into my back pocket for my mobile. Checking no one was around, I held it up in front of the picture and took a photo. Before I pressed send, I quickly tapped out a text to Marybeth.

URGENT! Show this to Mr W asap! Ask
him if 1 of the men is the piano tuner.
Lxx

If I was correct, and by now I was pretty sure I
was, then . . .

Chapter Nine

Half an hour later, we finally left the house. Even I had to admit it hadn't exactly been the most thrilling experience ever. Each room had been in a worse state than the last. The bathroom had been the worst of all. It stank of damp and there was even a frog that seemed to be living in the bath. I couldn't believe that anyone had ever paid good money to see it. Especially with Mme Lameme as the tour guide. Even without being able to understand what she was saying, it had been clear that she hadn't wanted us there. The others weren't even pretending to be interested; Jack kept giving me evils and even Mme Beaumont's smile was starting to look decidedly fixed. Plus I still hadn't heard back from Marybeth.

I sighed as we piled back into the car. Definitely not the best start to the holiday.

'Good one, Laurie,' Aimi muttered, as she clambered past me.

'Yeah,' muttered Jack. 'You owe us big time. What a waste of time.'

'Well, that's where you're wrong,' I started to say. 'I think I've found out . . .'

'Give it a rest, Laurie,' he said, rolling his eyes at the others. 'Just because our parents are detectives, it doesn't make you one. You've been watching too many episodes of *The Bill*.'

'But,' I said, 'I really think I'm on to something.'

'Save it,' he snapped, glaring at me. 'Nobody's interested.'

I looked at the others, but they all refused to meet my eyes. I could tell by the expressions on their faces it was pointless even trying to explain. We all fell into an awkward silence. Hurt, I stared out of the window, pretending not to care, as the car bounced back along the drive. Just then my phone beeped. Quickly, I checked the message.

Got the photo! Can't find Mr W
anywhere. Will show him asap when
I track him down. Will let you know.
MB xx

I snapped my mobile shut and let out a groan of frustration. Jack rolled his eyes and looked at me.

'What's up now?' he asked, sounding not in the least bit sympathetic.

'Look, I know you think it's just my imagination going into overdrive, but this is really serious. Jack, I need you to listen to me. Please.'

Jack frowned. 'You're not going to leave this alone, are you?' he said.

I shook my head, not trusting myself to speak.

'OK,' he sighed, leaning back in his seat and folding his arms. 'Let's hear it.'

I spoke quietly, not wanting to be overheard. If I couldn't persuade my own brother I was on to something, there was no way I could convince the others.

'I think the piano tuner who was pretending to

be Charles Morris was actually Jean-Paul. Don't you see? The housekeeper told us he's away abroad on business – I think his "business" is at the academy trying to track down that ring. He's obviously worked out that Philippe sent the ring with the piano. That's why he wants to take the piano away, so he can look for it properly without being interrupted.'

Quickly, I showed him the photo I'd sent to Marybeth. 'I'm pretty sure it's the same man I saw with Mr Walsh that day, but I didn't take much notice of him at the time, so I can't be sure. I've sent Marybeth a picture of the portrait so she could ask Mr Walsh if it was the piano tuner. But she can't find him. And now I'm starting to get worried. I mean, what happens if Jean-Paul discovers the box no longer holds the ring? We've seen his house; we know how desperate he is for money. Philippe's letter said that Jean-Paul wouldn't agree with his decision to give the ring to Ms Lang. Jack, I'm really scared that Ms Lang could be in real danger! And we're stuck here in France!'

By that point I'd forgotten about speaking quietly and I practically shouted the last bit. Elle, Aimi and Noah turned round to stare at us. Elle took one look at my face, and leaned forward to switch on the car radio. French music blared out.

'What's going on?' asked Aimi.

Jack looked at me. 'Laurie's got another one of her theories,' he said. My heart sank. It was hopeless. I obviously hadn't been able to convince him. I stared out of the window, biting my lip, trying to fight back tears.

'And I think she might be on to something,' he said, reaching out to pat my arm. 'Tell them, Laurie.'

For the first time in my life, I actually wanted to hug my brother. Leaning over, I gave him a huge smacker on the cheek.

'Arghh! Gerrof!' he moaned, wiping his cheek with his sleeve. 'Girls!' He rolled his eyes at Noah.

Quickly, I filled the others in. When I finished, they all stared at each other.

'Blimey,' said Aimi.

'Me too,' said Noah. Bless him, it doesn't matter how long he lives in England he'll never be able to work out what blimey actually means. Like I've said, the boy can be totally clueless.

Aimi raised her eyebrows at Noah. After all, she's not English either, but she's managed to figure out what blimey means!

'Just as well he's cute,' she mouthed. I grinned back at her. It was good to feel part of the gang again.

'What are we going to do?' asked Elle.

'I don't know,' I groaned.

'Text Marybeth again. Tell her to warn Ms Lang,' said Aimi.

Frantically, I typed out a text.

> Tell Ms Lang we think Jean-Paul is the piano tuner. Tell her to call the police.
> Lxx

My phone beeped almost straight away.

> On my way. Watch this space. MBxx

The five of us sat in silence, staring at my mobile, desperate for it to beep again. But a watched mobile never rings and it remained stubbornly silent. Mme Beaumont turned to look at us.

'But you're all so quiet. Aren't you excited to be on holiday?'

'Yes, of course,' Aimi answered. But her lacklustre reply hardly convinced Mme Beaumont who switched off the radio and turned to look at us. I grabbed at Jack's arm as the car swerved unnervingly across the road.

'That's enough of that noise. Laurie, you sing like an angel. And those songs of yours are much better than some of that rubbish I hear on the radio. Half-dressed girls singing about their humps or lumps or whatever nonsense it is. Why don't you sing something?'

'Um, I'm not really in the mood to sing, Mme Beaumont,' I said.

'Nonsense, don't be shy. I know Christophe would love to hear it, wouldn't you, darling?'

Christophe looked at her blankly.

'Come on, what's that really catchy one of yours? "All Aboard"? Sing that one.'

'She won't let up until you do.' Elle grimaced. 'You might as well. It'll pass the time.'

Shrugging, I half-heartedly started to sing 'All Aboard', with the others joining in on backing vocals and Noah tapping out a beat on the back of the seat in front of him. But for once in my life I couldn't lose myself in the music. My head was too full of what might be going on back in England. And, judging by the lacklustre efforts of my fellow band members, they all felt exactly the same way.

Suddenly, my phone beeped. To Mme Beaumont's surprise we all broke off as I hit the read-message icon.

Have shown Mr W. He's taken photo 2
Ms Lang. What shall I do? MBx

Without looking at the others, I typed a message and pressed send.

99

Hope we're not 2 late. Txt as soon as u
hear anythg!! x

But we didn't hear anything back. I couldn't settle.
Even being in Paris in the Beaumonts' beautiful
apartment couldn't cheer me up.

'Laurie, stop checking your mobile. You're
making the rest of us nervous!' said Aimi, who, it
has to be said, was looking pretty nervous herself.
She reached across the sofa and squeezed my hand
reassuringly.

'I can't help it,' I said. Two hours had passed and
we still hadn't heard anything from Marybeth. I
knew she'd text as soon as she had news, but the
wait was seriously playing with my head. I'd even
tried calling Ms Lang directly to warn her, but the
phone had just rung and rung.

'What if something really bad has happened?'
asked Elle, looking at me miserably. Her dark
brown hair was standing up on end where she
kept running her fingers through it, and she'd
bitten all the nail varnish off her thumbnail. Under

normal circumstances, Elle would never be found looking so unkempt. She's one of the most chic girls I know. I think it's because she's French. I shrugged helplessly and started frantically pacing up and down the living room.

'Stop it, Laurie,' moaned Jack, throwing a cushion at me. 'You're making me feel tired!'

'I can't,' I said. 'Anything could be happening at the academy and there's nothing we can do about it.'

'I know something that will cheer you up,' said Jack. 'What did the pony say to his mum when he had a sore throat?'

I shrugged.

'I'm a little hoarse!'

I stared at him.

'Get it? Little horse! Hoarse!' Jack started laughing so hard he nearly fell off the chaise longue he was lounging on.

'Jack!' I frowned at him, pursing my lips. 'This is no time for jokes. Who knows what's going on back at the academy!'

'You're right,' he said. 'This is no time for horsing around!' Clutching his stomach, he fell on the floor, spluttering with laughter.

'Hilarious,' I muttered.

'Is this a private party or can anyone join in?' asked Noah, coming into the room munching on a *pain au chocolat.*

'I'm trying to get old sour face over there to crack a smile,' said Jack.

'And I'm trying to get my brother to understand

that this isn't the time to be mucking around,' I said severely.

Noah grinned at Jack. 'I think a little humour is exactly what we need to take our mind off everything,' he said. 'And if it's bad jokes you're after, you've come to the right place.

He wasn't kidding. True to form, he rattled off a list of some of the worst jokes I've ever heard.

Noah's top five bad jokes:

1. *What happened when the cat ate a ball of wool?*
   She had a litter of mittens!

2. *What do dogs use to wash their hair?*
   Sham-poodle!

3. *What kind of fish do you only see at night?*
   Starfish!

4. *What do you give a sick pig?*
   Oink-ment!

5. What did the cuddling hedgehogs say?
Ouch!

They were so bad we were soon all laughing hysterically. Especially at Noah and Jack's efforts to explain them to Elle and Aimi. Noah's attempt to act out oink-ment had me snorting with laughter. He was right – his jokes did take my mind off what could be happening back at the academy. Anyway, call me shallow, but if your crush was going out of his way to make you laugh, you'd soon cheer up too.

'That's more like it,' said Mme Beaumont, coming into the room and finding us all completely helpless with laughter. 'I was starting to worry about you all. Dinner's ready.'

We all filed into the dining room. The food looked delicious – gorgeous pizzas oozing with cheese, and piles of garlic bread. Normally, I'd be tucking in, but tonight I couldn't eat a thing. I was too worried about Ms Lang. My heart was racing, my mouth was dry and I could barely breathe. The very thought of food made my stomach turn over. And not in a good way. The same couldn't be said for Jack and Noah who attacked the food like they hadn't eaten in a month.

'*C'est* delicious, *monsieur*,' Jack said, through a mouthful of garlic bread, spraying crumbs across the table.

'Nice manners,' I hissed sarcastically.

'Thanks, sis!' he winked.

I raised my eyes to the ceiling.

'Don't you like pizza, Laurie?' asked Mme Beaumont.

I thought I'd managed to do quite a convincing job of pretending to eat, while pushing food around my plate. But obviously not.

'I'm sorry, Mme Beaumont. It looks lovely, but I'm just not very hungry.'

Mme Beaumont put down her knife and fork and looked at me.

'Is there something going on I should know about?' she asked. 'You've all been acting strangely since we visited Montpellier House.'

I looked at Elle. She looked at her mum.

'The thing is . . .'

Just then, my mobile started vibrating in my pocket. Marybeth! At last! I glanced at the screen, but it wasn't Marybeth's name flashing at me. It was a London landline: The Verity Lang Academy! I flipped my phone open.

'Hello?' I said nervously.

'Laurie?' came a familiar voice.

I sat stunned for about three seconds, then shut

my eyes with relief. 'Ms Lang!'

I stood up, 'Excuse me,' I said to Mme Beaumont. 'I have to take this call, then I'll explain everything, I promise.'

I walked out of the room into the sitting room. It was only when I sank into an armchair, that I realised everyone had followed me, including Mme Beaumont and Christophe.

I spoke into the phone again, 'Hello, Ms Lang? Actually, there are quite a few people here who'd like to speak to you . . .'

Chapter Ten

Grinning at the others, I pressed speaker phone, so they could all hear.

'Ms Lang!' I said. 'I can't tell you how relieved I am to hear your voice. We've been going out of our minds with worry all day!'

It occurred to me too late that I was sounding a bit like her mother! Fortunately, she saw the funny side.

'I'm sorry, Laurie,' said Ms Lang. She sounded tired. 'But this is the first chance I've had to call. As you can imagine, I've been pretty busy all day!'

'I bet!' I said.

'Before I say anything else I want to say a big thank you for sticking to your guns about the piano tuner. As I said to you before, don't let anyone ever tell you not to listen to your instinct. It's a talent that should be nurtured, not ignored.'

'Don't worry, I always had faith in her, Ms Lang!' shouted Jack.

I kicked him in the shins.

'So I guess you're wondering what happened?' asked Ms Lang.

'Yes,' we all shouted. Even Mme Beaumont.

Ms Lang laughed down the phone. 'Well, as soon as I realised the key was missing, I wondered if the man calling himself Charles Morris could have taken it. I may be getting old, but I'm not yet losing my marbles and I knew I'd put it in that drawer. I didn't want to say anything to you, as I didn't want to worry you.'

'It takes more than that to worry me, Ms Lang,' I said.

'So I'm starting to realise, Laurie,' said Ms Lang.

I beamed down the phone.

'Anyway, after you showed me the box, I went straight back to the office and made a call to Morris and Co. to let them know someone had been posing as Charles Morris. But as neither they nor I had any further information there was nothing more we could do.

'Until of course Mr Walsh knocked on my door this afternoon with the picture you'd sent to Marybeth. Poor Mr Walsh. He didn't have a clue what was going on, although when Marybeth showed him the picture he recognised the man immediately as the piano tuner. And I recognised him as Jean-Paul, albeit an older version of the man I'd met many years earlier, when I first met Philippe.'

'I knew it!' I screeched down the phone.

'Laurie, I may be on the other side of the English Channel, but modern technology is a wonderful thing and there's no need to shout. I'm not deaf.'

I grinned at the others. Ms Lang may have been caught up in a sinister plot against her, but it'd take a lot more than that to ruffle her feathers.

'Sorry, Ms Lang,' I said. 'But what happened? Did you call the police? Have they caught Jean-Paul? It's been so frustrating being in France, knowing all this stuff is happening back home.'

'I'll let Marybeth tell you the rest of the story. She's here with me now. And I know she's got some other exciting news she's looking forward to telling you. Marybeth?'

There was a crackle as the phone changed hands.

'Hello? Laurie?'

'Marybeth!' I struggled to hold on to the phone as the others squeezed round it, desperate to talk to her.

'How are you?' I said.

'We miss you!' shouted Elle.

'We all do!' shouted Noah.

'Ah, thanks, guys,' said Marybeth. 'I miss you too.'

'So what happened after Ms Lang recognised the photo?' I asked.

'Well, I didn't know for ages. That's why I didn't text you. Sasha Quinn-Jones caught me in the corridor on my way back from Ms Lang's office.'

'So?' Jack said. 'It's half-term. It's not like you

need a hall pass to be out of lessons.'

'Oh, I know,' sighed Marybeth. 'I tried pointing that out. But you know what she's like.

'Sasha decided that I obviously didn't have anything constructive to do with my time, so she set me to work sorting out all the lost property that wasn't claimed last year. There was loads of it. It took me hours. She just sat there while I put everything into piles, making calls on her mobile and painting her nails.'

I grimaced down the phone. I could just imagine it.

'Someone really needs to take that girl down a peg or two,' I said grimly. 'Let's hope one of us gets her as a partner in one of Mrs D'Silva's trust exercises, where we have to fall back into each other's arms. We can accidentally-on-purpose drop her.'

'Too right,' said Aimi indignantly, scowling at the rest of us. 'That girl is completely out of order. She thinks she can do whatever she likes just because her parents are well off.'

'If you call filthy rich well off!' Jack laughed with a snort.

'Oh, it wasn't all bad,' Marybeth sighed. 'At least I found some tap shoes in my size. If no one claims them, that'll save Mom some serious money.'

I smiled. Typical Marybeth – she can find the silver lining in any situation.

'Plus, Ms Lang came looking for me and when she saw what was going on she wasn't impressed.'

'I bet,' said Noah.

'In fact, she told Sasha Quinn-Jones that as she was so determined to show such school spirit during the holidays there were a few more jobs that needed doing, and sent her off to help Mr Brown clean the drama studio. Her face was priceless! She stood there bleating like a lost sheep, "Baaah . . . baaah . . . but . . ."'

The rest of us burst out laughing at Marybeth's uncanny impression of Sasha Quinn-Jones's accent, and Jack and Noah high-fived.

'Brilliant,' said Elle. 'I can just see the look on her face.'

'It took every bit of acting talent I have not to smirk,' Marybeth giggled. 'I just smiled sweetly and asked Ms Lang what had happened with Jean-Paul.'

'And?' I asked.

'Well, the minute Ms Lang recognised the photo, she got straight on the phone to the police,' said Marybeth. 'They came to the academy right away and arrested Jean-Paul as soon as he turned up. I saw it all from the windows at the front of the building. It was so dramatic. I wish you'd been here to see it. It was brilliant! Apparently he's at the local police station in Lowfield being questioned as we speak.'

'I wish we'd been there, too,' I said.

'Mind you, if we had been, Laurie would never have seen that picture of Jean-Paul,' Noah said, putting his arm round my shoulder and giving me a quick squeeze.

Marybeth was still speaking, but I couldn't hear a word she was saying. All I could think was *Noah Hansen's put his arm round me.* Twice. In a week! My heart was pounding so hard, I couldn't hear anything else. I cleared my throat.

'Anyway, Marybeth, I really wanted to say thank you. I couldn't have done it without you. You're a total star.'

'You're welcome,' said Marybeth, and I could hear her grinning down the phone. 'But you can thank me in person tomorrow, because Ms Lang's paid for my ticket to France as a thanks for our help!'

I practically dropped the phone with excitement as everyone stamped and cheered. Noah and Jack were bouncing around the room, holding on to each other's arms.

'I take it you're quite pleased, then,' Marybeth shouted over the din.

'Oh, you know, just a bit!' I laughed. 'See you tomorrow. *Bon voyage.*'

I pressed end on my phone. As I placed it back in my pocket, I was floored by another of Jack's group hugs, but for once I didn't mind a bit.

The next evening, Mme Beaumont cooked up a real French feast as a celebration. Chicken in a rich sauce, plenty of *frites* and bread and the most delicious cheese I've ever tasted. Marybeth had arrived earlier that afternoon and the six of us had wasted no time in catching up and congratulating each other on solving another case.

After dinner, we all headed into the sitting room. Mme Beaumont suggested we put on one of our Lucky Six CDs, and this time we were soon all happily singing along. Even Christophe joined in, singing the chorus of 'All Aboard' with the rest of us, and doing some seriously good percussion with a fork and spoon.

'You'd better look out, Noah,' said Marybeth, grinning and nodding in Christophe's direction. 'I think you've got some competition!'

'I know!' he said, looking impressed as Christophe twirled the spoon round his wrist.

'Ah, don't worry,' said Elle. 'You'll always be our favourite drummer.'

'Definitely,' I said. 'Plus having one annoying

little brother in the band is more than enough.'

'Better than being a girly swot,' said Jack.

'Oh, great comeback!' I snorted.

'Swot!' said Jack.

'Wart-face!'

'It sure feels good to be back together!' laughed Marybeth.

I grinned back at her. I couldn't agree more.

FACT FILE   STAR SIGNS GUIDE TO...   BEAUTY

AIMI

NAME: Aimi Akita
AGE: 13
STAR SIGN: Leo
HAIR: Long, straight and black with two stylish blue streaks
EYES: Dark brown
LOVES: All the latest gadgets: laptop computers, MP3
players, mobile phones, webcams, and computer games.
As long as it's the newest must-have, she loves it! She
also loves her violin and her electric guitar
HATES: Outdated technology, being ignored and getting
dragged into Laurie's conspiracy theories
WORST CRINGE EVER: Organising a gig for the band before
they'd written any songs! Then having to own up – to the
band and the people at the venue

FACT FILE **STAR SIGNS** GUIDE TO... BEAUT

STAR HOBBIES

ARIES
You can use up your excess energy by playing a really physical sport. Football's always a good way of letting off steam. So get your kit on!

TAURUS
All Taureans love to sing – in shattering-chandelier style, preferably. So join your local amateur operatics society ASAP and get warbling! (Oh, and practise in the bath at every opportunity!)

GEMINI
You love chatting – in lots of different languages – so buying some foreign phrase books, or at least paying attention in French lessons, would be a good way of spending your spare time.

CANCER
You are the collector of the zodiac. You also like water and all that lives in it. So, if all your stamp albums are full, why not go fishing with a friend or relative?

LEO
You take your hobbies seriously and like to be the best at whatever you do. You have thespian tendencies, so taking some drama classes would be a good way of expressing your inner actress!

VIRGO
You like to do anything that involves using your hands. Pottery, knitting and making hand shadows are your favourite pastimes. Get practising!

LIBRA
You are a bit of a brain box, but would do well if you tried to get into a bit of physical activity now and again. Something aggressive yet dainty would suit.

SCORPIO
You like to concentrate, and can happily spend months making miniature replicas of St Paul's Cathedral from matchsticks and sweet wrappers!

SAGITTARIUS
You are the hunter of the zodiac. That's why you love to find old broken things on rubbish tips, then spend years repairing them. Oh, well, each to their own!

CAPRICORN
You spend all your spare time doing homework or something equally boffin-esque. Once the homework's done, you turn to the computer (in fact, you'd be on the computer 24/7 if you were allowed).

AQUARIUS
You are very kind and love to get involved in charity work. You enjoy doing stuff like campaigning or writing letters. Good for you!

PISCES
More than anything, you enjoy twirling around, toes pointed, arms akimbo, and would do well to join a dance class.

ARE YOU TURNING INTO YOUR MUM?

YOU MAY BE MORE LIKE HER THAN YOU REALISE . . .

1. DO PEOPLE TELL YOU THAT YOU LOOK LIKE YOUR MUM?
a) Sometimes
b) All the time
c) Never

2. WHICH OF THE FOLLOWING WOULD YOU CHOOSE TO DESCRIBE YOUR MUM?
a) She means well, but she gets on your nerves sometimes
b) She's great – the best mum in the world!
c) She's OK, but you don't like the way she treats you

3. DO YOU EVER BORROW YOUR MUM'S JUMPERS?
a) Only if all your own jumpers are in the wash
b) Never – even if they did fit, they'd look terrible
c) Yes – you have very similar taste in clothes

4. YOUR BEST FRIEND'S FAILED HER EXAMS AND IS REALLY UPSET. DO YOU:
a) Use some of your mum's wise advice to comfort your friend
b) Have advice at the ready. You know how to deal with these situations
c) Feel a bit awkward and mumble that you don't really know what to do or say, but do the best you can?

POP　　　　FUN　　　　QUIZ　　　　GAMES

6. HOW MANY OF THE FOLLOWING HAVE YOU FOUND YOUR-SELF DOING IN THE LAST MONTH? (Tick the ones you've done)

- Cringed at one of your mum's jokes
- Groaned when she put on her favourite 'sounds'
- Stifled a snigger at her new hairstyle
- Disagreed with one of her little pearls of wisdom

NOW ADD UP YOUR SCORES.

(If you chose answer A to question 1, for example, you score 2)

	A	B	C
1.	2	3	1
2.	2	3	1
3.	2	1	3
4.	3	2	1

5. Subtract one point for each one you've ticked (maximum of 4)

CONCLUSIONS

If you scored 0–4, you're YOU and nothing like your mum at all. There's no chance of you turning into your mum whether you look like her or not. You have completely opposing views on life, the universe and everything.

If you scored 5–8, you're ON THE TURN. You may find yourself speaking and thinking in similar ways to her. Lucky for you, your mum is a very nice person. And so are you.

If you scored 9–12, you're AS ONE. You have loads in common and share everything, from jackets to opinions. You sound like her, act like her and, chances are, you look like her too. You're like peas in a pod.

POP GAMES

MAKE A DULL EVENING MUSICALLY FUN-TASTIC
BY PLAYING THESE POP GAMES WITH YOUR
FAMILY AND FRIENDS!

NAME THAT TUNE!

How to play:

1) Ask each person to bring a few of their favourite CDs

2) Appoint one person as the DJ

3) This person must set the stopwatch the moment they start playing the CD, then, without telling the other players what it is, play the first 10 seconds of it

4) All the players must try to work out what the song is. As soon as someone shouts out the song and artist the stopwatch is stopped and checked

5) Subtract the number of seconds from 10 and put this number down as this player's score. So, for example, if after 7 seconds a player shouts out the correct answer, she scores 10 minus 7 = 3 points.

6) If no one gets the answer in 10 seconds, the DJ moves on to the next track

7) Continue this way until one track has been played from each CD

8) The winner is the person with the highest score

BE THE HOST OF A TV POP SHOW!

Anyone can host a TV pop programme . . . Can't they? Give it a go and see how you'd do!

1) Each player should imagine that they're in charge of a new pop show

2) Grab a pen and paper and write down who you'd invite to the studio to play and why

3) If you could interview a pop star on the show, who would you choose? Why do you think they'd be of interest to your viewers?

4) Which three new videos would you show?

5) Is there anything you could add to the show to improve it? (When TOTP first began in the 1960s, there were prizes awarded to the best dancer in the audience and the best-dressed member of the audience! Do you think that would work on your show?)

6) Think of a name for your show and design a logo for it

7) Get together with the other players and try to put a programme together between you using some of the best group ideas.

8) Decide who's best for which role in your programme. You'll need a presenter, scriptwriter and director.

Have fun!

MAKE YOUR OWN MOISTURISERS USING THE CONTENTS OF THE KITCHEN CUPBOARD!

NUTS 4 U!

For skin as smooth as a baby's bottom, make this moisturiser with minimum ingredients and fuss*

YOU'LL NEED:

- A cup
- Some warm water
- A packet of ground almonds
- A small bowl
- A sieve or strainer
- A fork
- A bottle

WHAT TO DO:

1. Pour one cup of warm water over four tablespoons of ground almonds in a small bowl

2. Push through a seive with a fork to create a milky-coloured liquid

3. Use after cleansing and toning as a luxurious moisturiser. Don't rinse it off – just let it soak into your skin

4. Keep it in the fridge in a bottle between uses

* Please avoid this recipe if you have a nut allergy

Chapter One

As schools go, The Verity Lang Academy for the Performing Arts is pretty cool. As well as having all the normal classes, like English, maths, science and so on, we study music, dance and drama, too. It means you're surrounded by people who are into the same things you are, and who are dedicated to being the best at what they do. Like our band, Lucky Six, which is pretty good, even if I do say so myself. If it weren't for school, we'd never have met. In fact, the only bad thing about the academy is that my younger brother, Jack, is here too . . .

'Get off me!' Jack yelled, shoving me to the other side of the car.

'You started it!' I shouted back.

'Kids!' yelled Mum. 'Quiet! Honestly, anyone would think you were both five years old. I'm so glad the holidays are over. Look, here's the school now.' She turned left and drove through the smart gates.

But where we'd been expecting to see a quiet sweeping driveway we saw instead hundreds of cars all ground to a halt and hordes of people milling about in confusion.

That shut us up.

'What's going on?' I wondered aloud.

'I hope there's nothing wrong,' Mum said anxiously. 'I have to get straight back to the station.' My parents are police officers, which is really cool when you want advice on thinking logically and following clues, but no good at all when you want to get them to agree to something. They can see right through you.

'I'll find out!' Jack offered, opening his door and disappearing.

'Me too!' I said. 'I want to find the others anyway.' I unclipped my seat belt.

'Wait!' Mum called. 'Look, take your suitcases. I'm afraid I can't wait. Call me if there's a problem.'

I helped Mum get our luggage out of the boot and kissed her goodbye. Then I charged off towards the crowd, eagerly scanning it for a familiar curly brown head belonging to a certain drummer called Noah. I had no luck, but I did spot a girl with a dark brown bob and brown eyes coming towards me.

'Elle!' I shrieked, running towards her and hugging her. 'It's so good to see you! How was France?'

'Oh, you know, same as ever,' Elle said, shrugging her shoulders while hugging me back. 'Did you have a good time in the Lake District?'

I nodded. 'Yeah, we did loads of hiking . . .' I began.

Suddenly we heard a voice calling my name. 'Laurie!' We turned round and there was Noah, tall and curly haired as ever.

'Hi!' I said, trying to sound cool. My heart was thumping really loudly and Elle must have heard it because she grinned at me like a maniac.

'What did you do this holiday, Noah?' I asked, trying to cover my blushes.

'Oh, you know,' he said lazily, slinging his bag down on the grass. 'Games, surfing, the usual.' Noah's parents are Greg Hansen and Michelle Albright, the Hollywood stars, and they have homes in New York and LA. Sounded like Noah had been in LA this holiday.

'Hey, guys!' Aimi yelled, waving at us over the heads of a group of year sevens. She disappeared behind them and then reappeared, dragging Marybeth behind her. Aimi's our feisty lead guitarist and Marybeth plays keyboards. Did I mention I write the songs and am the lead singer, with Elle on backing vocals? Elle's also our manager and publicist. Slowly, our band was coming together after the long summer break.

Jack was following Aimi and Marybeth. I shouldn't have been surprised – he follows Aimi everywhere. Unfortunately, Jack is also in Lucky Six. He's our bassist.

We all hugged each other.

'Lucky Six is back together!' I crowed, delighted.

'But what on earth is going on here?' Elle said, looking round in despair at the chaos. For Elle, Miss Neat-and-Tidy, it was like a horror film.

'Haven't you heard?' Aimi said. 'An old set of pipes burst this morning. Everything's flooded and loads of stuff has been damaged.'

We all gasped.

'We can't go in,' Marybeth explained. 'It's too dangerous. So that's why everyone's out here.'

'Wow!' I said. 'So what's going to happen?'

'We don't know yet,' Aimi shrugged.

'It's so good to see you all, though,' I said. I hugged the girls again. It felt like we'd been apart for ages.

At that moment, Sasha Quinn-Jones, year-nine prefect and total witch, brushed past us.

'I don't know why you're so excited,' she muttered.

Oh, no. She was *not* going to ruin my happiness at seeing everyone again. 'Well, I don't suppose *you'd* understand,' I snapped at her. 'But I'm just really happy to see my friends.'

Sasha stopped and looked at me patronisingly. 'Well, make the most of it,' she said sweetly. 'Because the flood is sure to mean school is closed and we'll all have to go home.'

We looked at each other in horror. Go home? We couldn't be separated for any longer! We needed to practise!

Just then, Ms Lang appeared at the front doors of the school looking very serious. Everyone shushed and fell silent. Her face was white and strained, but although this was a moment of crisis, I couldn't help admiring how chic she looked even in a pair of wellies.

'Good morning, everyone,' Ms Lang said, her clear voice ringing out over the crowd of students. 'I must apologise for the state of the school – this is no way to start a term. However, I'm afraid it's beyond our control at the moment. There's a lot of serious damage and a lot of hard work will be needed to get the building back into shape. There's no way we can use it as a school at present.'

There was a huge groan at this point. Noah and I looked at each other anxiously.

Ms Lang held up her hand for silence and the chattering died away again. 'I am pleased to say that two local schools have agreed to help us out. You will be split between these comprehensives. The day pupils will, of course, live at home as usual, and some boarders will stay with them, but the rest of you will have to stay with families of the comprehensive-school students. Any parents who are not happy with the plan should come and discuss it with me straight away.'

There was more muttering at this, but Ms Lang continued. 'Everyone has been very kind in offering to help us in our hour of need, and it won't be for long as the builders are starting work here straight away.' There was a cheer. 'But there's one important point: I'm afraid that the schools don't have the facilities we do – or did – and so you will only be studying the traditional school curriculum.'

'We ought to be able to take our instruments,

costumes and performing gear with us, though, Ms Lang,' came a posh voice from the crowd. Sasha. Of course.

Ms Lang's lips tightened at that. 'I would remind you, Miss Quinn-Jones, that these families are doing us a huge favour,' she said. 'They cannot be expected to accommodate all your equipment and costumes as well. Besides, I'm sorry to say that some of these have been damaged and until we sort out the insurance, there won't be enough of anything to go round.'

Marybeth gave a sudden sob. 'Our instruments!' she whispered.

'Typical,' Aimi fumed. 'I take my violin home to practise for my parents, and leave my guitar here to get ruined!'

We looked at each other in despair. It seemed *everything* was ruined.

A few hours later, we were all gathered in the

main hall. It had been drained of water but was in a terrible mess. Lucky Six all stood together as Ms Lang arrived on the stage.

'OK, everyone,' she said. 'We've sorted out who's going to which school. It's been done randomly as there wasn't time to ensure groups of friends stayed together. It's been hard enough as it is so I don't want to hear any complaints or requests for swaps.' She looked hard in our direction at this point. My heart sank. 'It's not for long,' Ms Lang continued. 'You'll just have to make the most of it.'

Elle and I looked at each other. Surely they wouldn't split Lucky Six up?

'These are the students going to Bank Lane Comprehensive,' Ms Lang said. She started reading out a list of names. '. . . Elle Beaumont . . . James Dixon . . . Marybeth Fellows . . . Jack Hunt . . . Sarah Matthews . . . Dan Piper . . . Sasha Quinn-Jones . . .'

We were ticking the band off on our fingers. That was half of us! Only three more to go. But then she stopped.

'And here are the students going to Larkfield Comprehensive,' Ms Lang said. 'Aimi Akita . . . Rufus Donovan . . . Robin Ferguson . . . Noah Hansen . . . Laurie Hunt . . . Olivia McCallum . . . Zoe Morrison . . .'

That was all of us. We gazed at each other in horror. We were split up! And not only that – the two schools were miles away from each other! Lucky Six had been torn apart!

While you wait for your next
Lucky Six fix, why not feast your eyes
on our *Megastar Mysteries* series?

Here's a sneak preview of book one for starters . . .

Mirage

AVAILABLE NOW
from all good bookshops, or
www.mega-star.co.uk

Chapter One

OK, I have a confession to make. None of this would have happened if I hadn't bunked off school. Now don't get me wrong, I honestly don't make a habit of skipping school. And all I missed is lunch and then drama. It's the school play in three weeks' time, which means everyone is pretty much caught up in full rehearsal mode. That's great if you've got a good part, but I've been given the part of – wait for it – a tree swaying gently in the breeze. As you can probably guess, it doesn't exactly call for huge acting ability. That's not why

I'm bunking off, though. Seriously, I love trees and I'm not petty like that. I had decided if I was going to be a tree then I was going to be the best tree that Whitney High School had ever seen. I even went to the park and studied different types of trees – that's how dedicated I am. But last night, when I was doing my English homework, Abs' instant messaging name flashed up on my computer.

> **CutiePie:** Guess what?
> **NosyParker:** What?
> **CutiePie:** Mirage Mullins is opening Top Choonz. Tomorrow.
> **NosyParker:** You lie.
> **CutiePie:** Au contraire, mon frère. Between 1.30 p.m. and 2.30 p.m.

Mirage is HUGE. Her first single has been number one for weeks and weeks and weeks. Her video is seriously hot, too. The girl is *totally* cool. And me, Abs and Soph are her biggest fans *ever*. I've read every single article ever written about her and pretty much know everything there is to know about her, from what she has for breakfast (strawberry yoghurt and fruit, in case you were wondering) to her most embarrassing moment (when she fell over on stage, revealing her knickers to hundreds of her fans).

NosyParker: WE HAVE TO SEE HER!
CutiePie: YEP!
NosyParker: So what's the plan, Stan?
CutiePie: Meet you and Soph at the bus stop 1 p.m. Don't get caught, OK?
NosyParker: OK!

So that's how I was heading towards Top Choonz with Abs and Soph at 1.15 p.m. instead of going to drama rehearsal. Even if you hadn't heard a new music store was about to open in town, you wouldn't have been able to miss it. There were life-size pictures of Mirage in every single window and huge signs everywhere saying, 'Official Opening Today'.

The atmosphere inside the shop was buzzing. There was already a humongous queue. All around us there were girls clasping posters and CDs, chattering excitedly. There were at least seven other people who should have been at drama rehearsal (Mr Lord, our drama teacher, was so not going to be happy.) I even heard one man in a business suit nudge his friend and say, 'I'm going to get her autograph and sell it on the Internet.'

Just then, a ripple of excitement went through the queue as a sleek black limousine pulled up in front of the shop.

'This is it! This is it!' squealed Soph, hopping eagerly from one foot to another.

I was so excited I could hardly breathe. I'd been dreaming for so long about actually meeting Mirage Mullins and now it was going to happen.

For a split second there was silence as Mirage – looking totally gorgeous in a shocking-pink catsuit – slipped out of the limo, dwarfed by four burly security guards. Then, as one, the queue surged forward. The security guards shouted into their radios, while fending off the hands of grasping fans, desperate to touch their idol, all screaming, 'Mirage! Mirage! MIRAGE!!!'

'This is crazy!' I shouted above the noise to Abs and Soph.

Abs winked back at me. 'Yeah. I wouldn't have missed it for the world!' she shouted.

The three of us grinned goofily at each other. This was sooo much better than drama rehearsals. I looked at Mirage. She didn't seem scared or anything, which I would have been if I was in her shoes. She simply made her way to the front of the queue and calmly addressed the screaming crowd.

'You can all have an autograph. Just one at a time, OK?'

But no one was listening. Girls were thrusting pens and CDs at her from all sides and one woman, who looked about the same age as my mum, had thrown herself at Mirage's leg and was crying, 'I love you, Mirage. I LOVE YOU!' It was crazy. In fact I was starting to get a bit scared, especially as the girls nearest Mirage were leaping towards her as if they wanted to pull her clothes right off her body. Which is so not the way to ingratiate yourself with your idol, let me tell you.

Just as I was beginning to panic that I was going to get flattened by the crowd, three things happened at once. The security guards made a human wall around Mirage. The manager of the shop appeared and cleared his throat, before making a speech to thank Mirage for officially opening the store. And thirdly, out of the corner of my eye I spotted a familiar figure . . .

'Mum!' I hissed, ducking down behind the man in front, pulling Abs and Soph with me. The three of us watched in horror as Mum made her way into the store. She must have been on her lunch break from the council offices where she works, passed the store, heard the commotion and wandered in to see what was going on. I practically stopped breathing as she headed towards us. No way would Mum understand that the chance to meet Mirage Mullins was more important than being at school.

'What are we going to do?' I whispered frantically at Abs and Soph. 'She can't spot us. She'll kill me!'

Abs and Soph had turned scarily pale.

'We'll be grounded for life,' Abs hissed back.

I looked around wildly, desperately searching for an escape route. A few more steps and she'd be practically on top of us. Suddenly, I spotted a huge display of CDs towards the back of the store. Manically, I signalled the other two and got ready to push my way through the shrieking throng.

'Go! Go! GO!' I shouted and ran as if my life depended upon it. Which, knowing my mum, it pretty much did.

Out of breath, I collapsed behind the display. 'Did she see us? Did she see us?' I gasped at the other two.

Soph peered out.

'I don't think so,' she whispered. 'She's looking at some CDs.'

Cautiously, I raised my head to look. Mum had a CD called *Best of the Eighties* in her hand and was making her way towards the till. I honestly never thought the day would come when I would be grateful for Mum's totally embarrassing taste in music.

We waited until Mum had wandered out of the shop and was out of sight before getting up and sighing with relief. Then we headed back to the queue, which had thinned out considerably.

Mirage was now sitting at a table, signing CDs and posing for photos. She had a smile and a few words for every single fan, but even from where I was standing I could see the smile never quite touched her eyes. I felt for her, I really did. I've seen enough reality shows like *Newlyweds/The Osbournes/Girls Aloud Off The Record* and so forth to know how hard it must be when you're a megastar and you have to be nice to everyone all the time, even if you've got the worst toothache ever, or you've just had bad news, like your nan's been rushed into hospital, but you can't show you're upset, just in case someone thinks you're not a nice person and stops buying your records. I was determined to be extra nice to Mirage when it came to my turn and to let her know just how much her fans appreciated all her hard work.

It seemed like an age before, at long last, we were next in the queue. A few more steps and I'd be able to touch her. I could hardly stand still with excitement.

Suddenly, a huge security guard blocked our way. What the crusty old grandads!

'Sorry, girls,' he said. 'That's all Mirage has time for today.'

We stared at him in disbelief. 'But that's not fair,' gasped Soph. 'We've queued for over an hour.'

'We're her biggest fans in the world,' added Abs.

'PLEEEEEASE!' we all begged in unison.

But the security guard was completely unmoved. 'Sorry, girls,' he shrugged. 'Mirage has to leave.'

No way was I going to get this far and not meet my idol. No, siree. Not me. Before the security guard could realise what was happening, I'd ducked past him.

'I'm sorry,' I gasped as I ran towards a shocked-looking Mirage. 'But I just had to meet you. I just wanted to tell you that I think you're great.'

Mirage looked nervously at the security guard, who was already bearing down on us and was, I noticed, looking pretty mad.

'I don't normally behave like this!' I gabbled. 'I just had to meet you.'

Mirage glanced at her security guard again, then quickly reached out and grabbed my hand, shaking it up and down like her life depended on it. 'I'm very glad you did,' she said, still pumping my hand up and down. 'Very glad.'

I didn't have a chance to say anything else, as right then the security guard grabbed me by the scruff of my neck, lifted me right off my feet, slung me over his shoulder and carried me out of the store. It was only after he'd literally dropped me on the pavement and walked back inside the store that I realised I was holding a scrunched-up note in my hand. Completely confused, I flattened it out, then stared at the words in disbelief.

Collect all
the titles in the series

Available from all good bookshops
www.mega-star.co.uk